# OUR LITTLE SECRET

K. LUCAS

EBook ISBN: 978-1-958445-03-7

Paperback ISBN: 978-1-958445-01-3

Hardback ISBN: 978-1-958445-02-0

*Editing and Proofreading by My Brother's Editor*

*For my readers*

# OUR LITTLE SECRET

A NOVELLA

Bestselling Author

# K. LUCAS

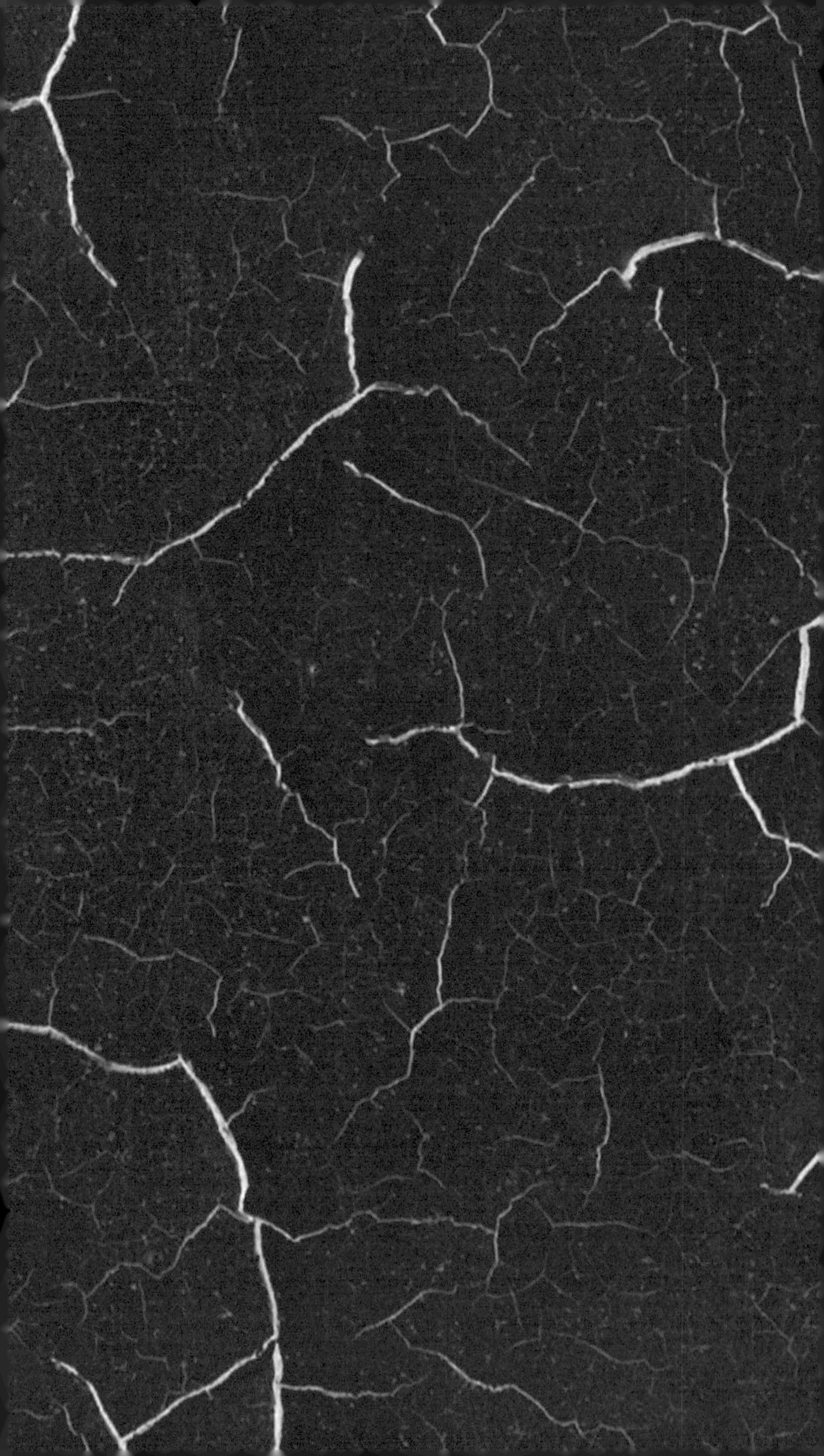

# MITCH

## Now

Tomorrow's the day. It's so close I can almost *taste* it. After *five* miserable years, I'm finally going to be free. I smile to myself, relishing the idea of all the things I'm going to do when I'm out of this fucking place *at last*.

I brace myself for another push-up, let my body go down toward the floor, push up, go down again, and then up once more. I repeat the movements until my arms burn, then I move into a sit-up position. I brace my hands behind my head and go through the movements, thinking about tomorrow.

Footsteps come from down the hall. "Mail call, Mitch," the guard calls, stopping outside my cell.

"Thanks," I say, getting up to take the envelope from through the bars. *Another returned letter.* I crumple it into a ball and throw it against the wall, watching it land in the toilet.

I grind my jaw, imagining my hand around someone's

throat instead of paper. *One more day, baby. You can tell me how sorry you are.*

If there's one thing I've learned from being here, it's patience. *The best things in life are worth waiting for,* isn't that what they say? And *she* is worth it. *Revenge* is worth it, too.

I take a few deep breaths to calm my nerves. Then I sit down with a fresh sheet of paper to try again. This will be the last letter I write while in this facility. It's a refreshing thought.

I smile to myself, feeling better already.

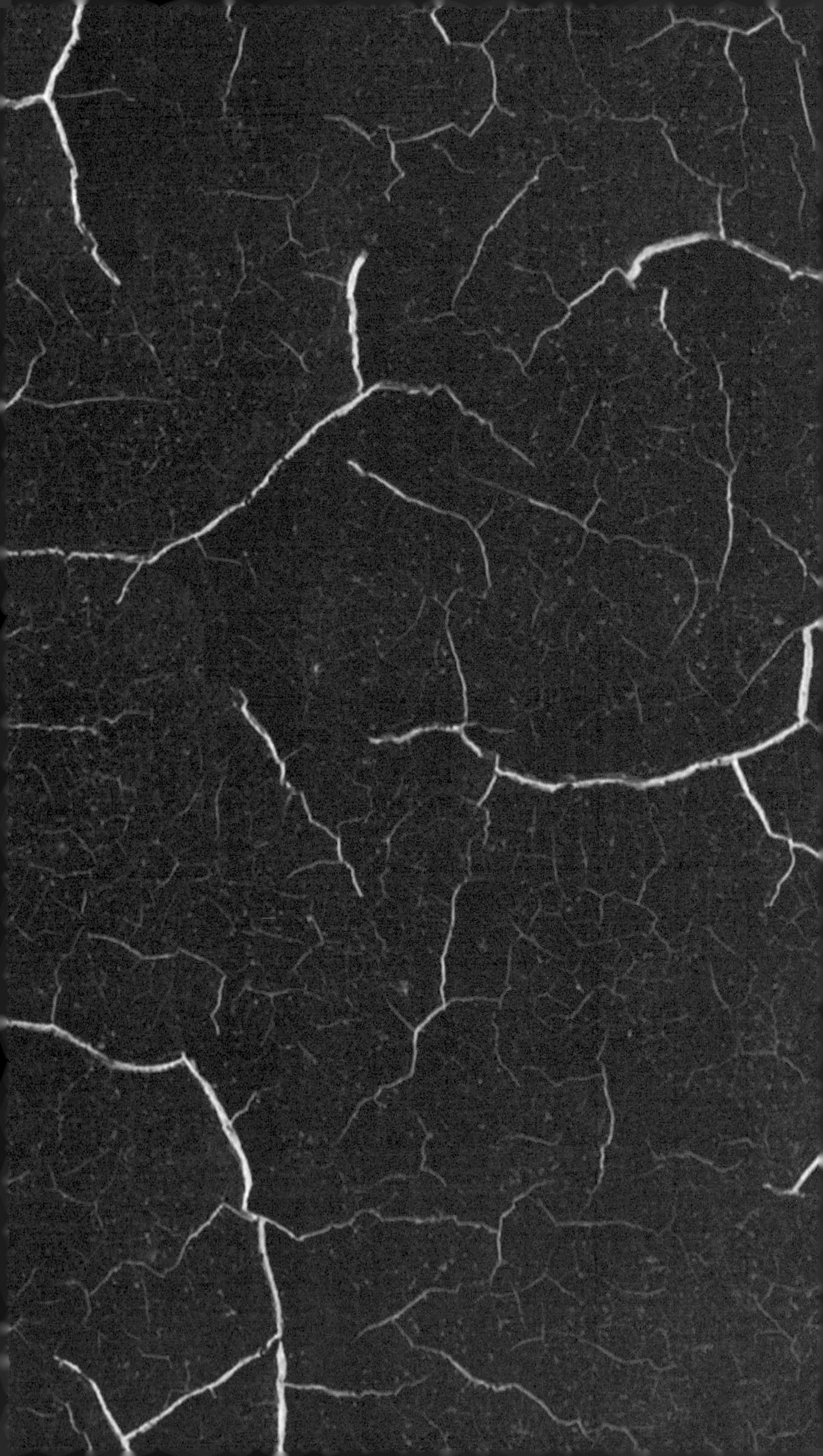

2

———

MITCH

*Now*

SHE'S SO BEAUTIFUL. God, what an idiot I was—am, for letting her get away. Five years and she hasn't aged a day. Her hair has gotten longer, darker too, somehow. It was black before, but now it's blacker—glossier and straighter.

I had a picture of her in my mind while I was locked away. It pulled me through, kept me holding on. I saw her through everything I did, every list I made, every piece of the plot that went together.

An image of her naked, smiling face comes to mind now. *I wrap a wavy strand of her hair around my finger, tracing it down the length of her. She wants to scratch at the little strands that brush across her skin, but I stop her, blowing on them to make them move some more.*

I shake off the image. It won't do me any good right now. Not yet.

It wasn't hard to find her here—almost like she was just waiting for me. A diner, not a nice restaurant but still, *like before.* My heart races at the thought. *Has she been waiting for me all this time?*

"Table for one?" the hostess says, greeting me at her podium. They're busy today—Sunday morning church crowd, but that's how I wanted it.

"Yeah, thanks," I say, smiling at her.

I wipe my damp hands against my jeans as she leads me to a booth by the window. I think I might get lucky, might be placed in her section of the diner, but not today. She's where all the families are—all the children. My throat closes at the thought.

I take a deep breath. *I may not be in her section, but I have the perfect view.* Sipping my coffee, pretending to read my book, I watch while she helps other customers. It's all about patience.

An hour ticks by and then another. I flip the pages of my novel, pretending to scan the pages. I force myself to sip the coffee so when the server comes he has something to refill.

I can't stay too long, or I'll be noticed. I'm not ready for that yet, so grudgingly, I leave. *It's okay*, I remind myself, *It's all part of the plan.*

There's nothing else on my to-do list, so I decide to stick around the area—for four more hours—until I see that beautiful face walk out the front door. My heart rate picks up again. *It's been so long.*

I watch as Raven adjusts her purse over her shoulder and fiddles with her keys. She surprises me by pressing her key fob to unlock a brand-new-looking car. A *Jaguar,* for crying out loud!

My fists clench around the steering wheel of my beater, squeezing until my knuckles pop. There's no way she can afford that car working at a diner—not even if she's the manager. No. There's only one explanation, and I'm going to confirm it.

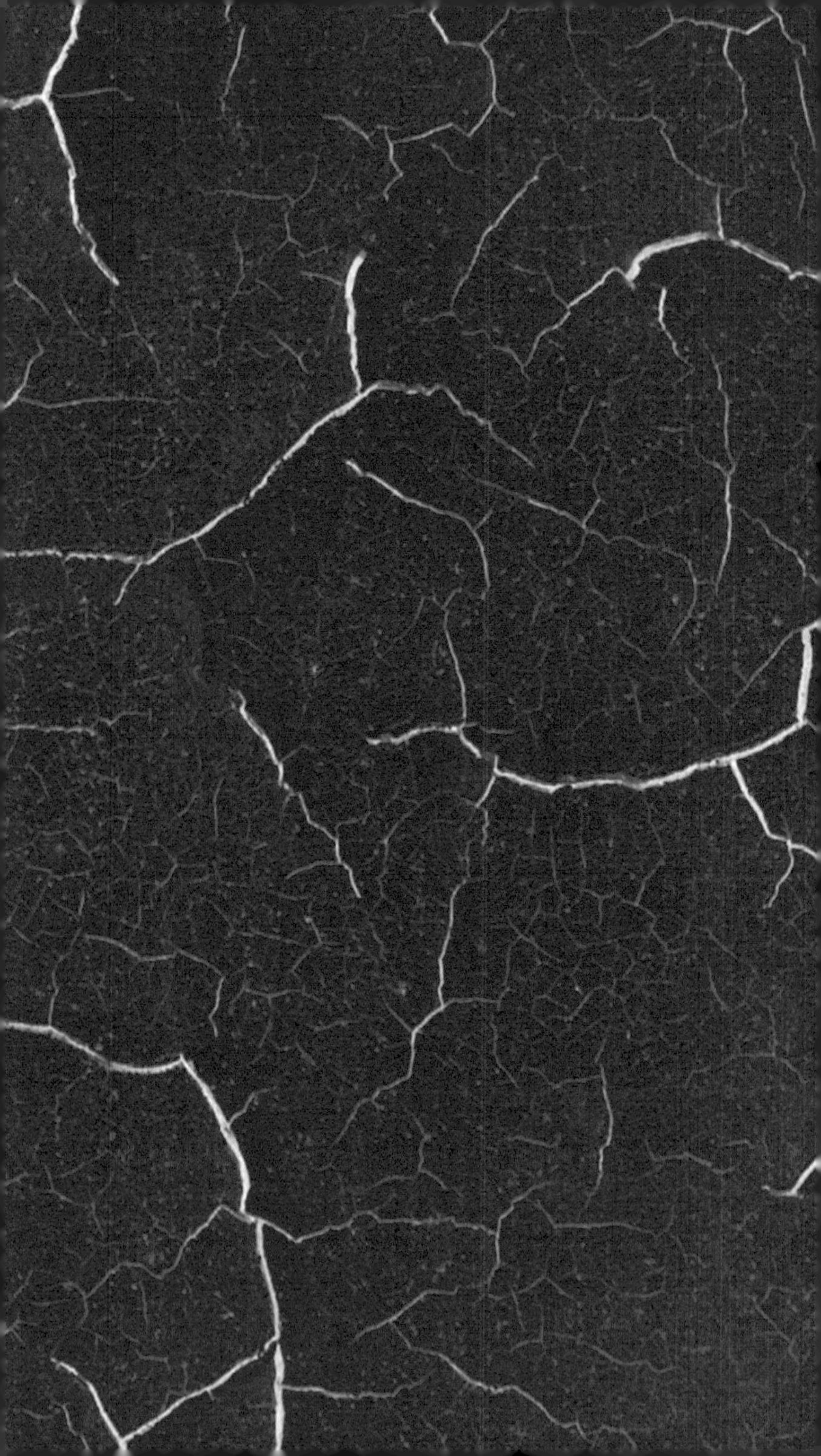

3

———

RAVEN

Then

Wiping my sweaty palms against my pants, I reach for the door handle and step into the air-conditioned restaurant. It's busy, even at this time of day, when I thought for sure it would be dead—too late for lunch, too early for dinner. *Goes to show how much I know.*

"I'm here for a job interview," I say to the hostess.

She raises an eyebrow at me, probably wondering who on earth would do an interview when they were that busy. When I don't say anything else, she asks, "Do you know who it's supposed to be with?"

"Mitch, I think."

"I'll go get him. One sec."

I sit in the waiting area, feeling the eyes of everyone on me. Families are sitting here, waiting to be seated, their kids restless. I fan myself with my résumé, trying not to crinkle the paper.

"Nervous?" the lady next to me asks, smiling

"Yes," I say, giving a small smile back.

"Your first time working in a restaurant?"

I nod.

"You have a friendly smile," she says. "You'll do well. Don't put up with difficult customers, they're not worth it."

"I—thank you."

I try not to squirm in my seat. *Difficult customers?* I didn't think about that before applying. I just thought that I needed a job, needed money, hopefully doing something that didn't bore me to tears or that I hate. *Maybe I should've thought a little harder about this particular trade.*

"Raven?"

I look up to see a man in his late thirties, maybe early forties, scan the waiting area with expectant eyes. There's a single moment where I think *I could just walk out the door.* I don't know why I think it—I wanted the job, I'm here to get it, but I'm somewhat disturbed now, even if it's for no reason.

"That's me," I say, standing up with a smile. I reach to shake his hand. "It's nice to meet you."

"Mitch. Nice to meet you, Raven."

He leads me through to an *employees-only* area, where he has a small private office. He ushers me through the door before closing it behind me.

"I appreciate your patience. We're unexpectedly busy today. A little short staffed," he says with a smile.

"It's no problem. I'm glad to wait."

He chuckles and I blush at the double meaning of my own words.

"Tell me a little bit about yourself, Raven. I'd love to get to know you a little."

*I hate this question so much.* What does he really

want to know? Does he want to hear my literal life story—where I grew up, how many siblings I have? Or is he talking more about job experience? I'm too uncomfortable to share anything personal, so I decide to stick with job experience.

I admit to him the lack of experience I have in the restaurant industry, but also talk about my eagerness to learn and apply myself. We discuss volunteer work I've done in the past with food service, and half an hour passes without me even noticing.

"I'd love to offer you the job," Mitch finally says.

"Really? Thank you so much!" I can't believe he's actually offering the job on the spot. I thought for sure he'd have to consult another manager, or the owner, or someone else.

He grins at me. "When can you start?"

"Right away. Tomorrow if you need."

Mitch nods. "I like your enthusiasm. The weekly schedule gets drawn up tomorrow. I'll have your name added and we'll get going from there. Expect a phone call soon."

"That sounds great. Thank you so much, Mitch. I won't let you down." I stand up and reach my hand out to shake his again.

He takes mine in his, giving me a gentle shake. He holds on to me for a minute, smiling a little too brightly. His eyes darken and a chill runs up my spine.

"Well, I'll see you soon," I say, tugging my hand away.

He lets me go. I leave his office and the restaurant without another word.

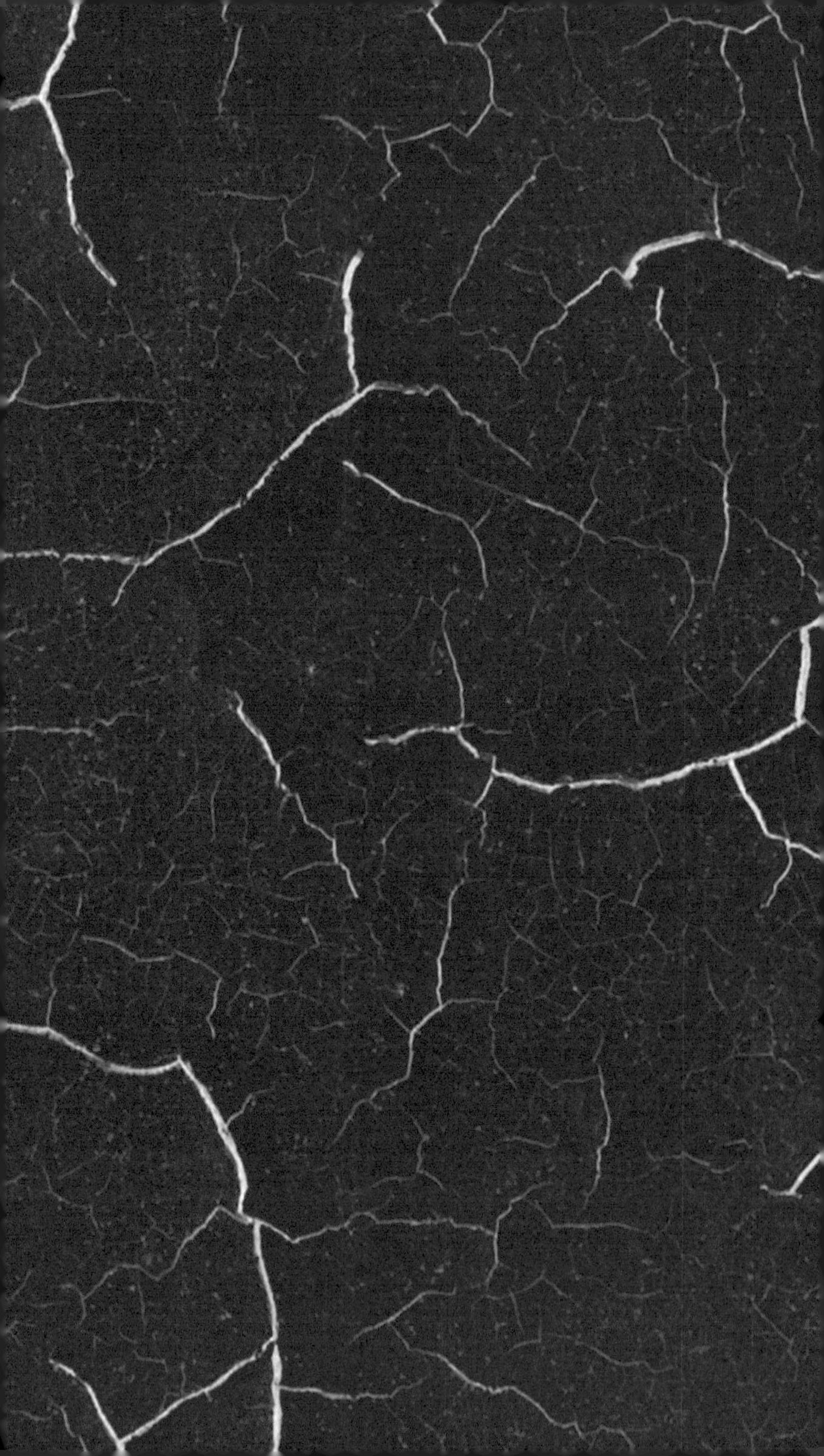

# 4

# MITCH

## Now

I FOLLOW as Raven weaves through traffic, speeding around cars effortlessly. It's harder for me to keep up at times—she drives like a bat out of hell, but it keeps me on my toes. When she gets too far ahead, I roll down my window and listen to the roar of her engine to tell me which way she's gone.

It's not hard to find her. It never is. Besides—there are only so many places she can go, and this city isn't *that* big. If push comes to shove, I can always wait for her at home.

She pulls into a gym parking lot. I think about following her inside but decide to wait for now. *I might have to get a membership of my own soon enough.*

Raven spends an hour and a half inside. When she walks back through the doors, her hair is wet. A towel is draped over her shoulders and she's sucking on a straw.

My eyes are glued to her, the image so erotic, I couldn't look away if I tried. I'm taken back to before—a time when we were in the shower together, and she was sucking on something else. My mouth goes dry.

She climbs into her car, breaking my trance. I shake my head. *Focus, Mitch.*

Onward we drive, swerving in and out of traffic again. I'm thankful to have something else to concentrate on as I press the accelerator harder. *I wonder if she can feel me watching her.* I smile at the thought. *Maybe that's why she's driving so fast.*

---

A GROCERY STORE IS NEXT. This time, I do follow her in. I'm helpless to resist.

I grab a cart on my way in through the sliding doors, trying to act casual. I'm wearing a hat that covers my face, but I wonder if it will do any good. She might not recognize me anyway—five years is a long time, especially five years in prison.

But another part of me, a hopeful part, wonders if she might know me anyway. Maybe she'd be able to pick me out of a lineup even if she was half-blind and I was in disguise. She would just *feel* me.

"Excuse me, sir?" a voice says, making me jump.

I turn to see an elderly woman standing next to me. I smile. "Can I help you?"

"I'm so sorry to bother you," she says. "Would you mind helping me with this water?"

"Of course," I say, trying not to grind my teeth. *Raven is getting away.* I pull the case of water off the shelf and put it in her shopping cart. She smiles her thanks and I take off down the aisle before she can ask me to reach the prune juice.

It's an effort to blend in with everyone else, walking so damn *slow*. I fight the urge to run through the aisles until I find her again. *I have to keep it casual.*

I finally find her again in the produce, examining apples. I swallow the lump in my throat. *This is it.*

I pause. *Am I really going to just waltz right up to her?* I turn and pretend to look at the bananas. *Shit.* I haven't thought this through enough—well, I have, I've thought it through for five fucking years, but I haven't *planned* enough.

Raven's phone rings. I stay away, still not ready to be seen. But I can't resist the temptation, so I stay close enough to hear her end of the conversation.

"Hey," she says. "I'm just picking up some groceries."

She waits, listens for a minute, then says, "I thought you were picking her up."

A sigh. "No. I'm sorry, it's my fault."

"It's no problem. I'm around the corner anyway."

"Yes, I'm sure."

She laughs. "I love you too."

My heart stops. Raven turns and I get a better look at the hand holding her phone. There's an engagement ring on her finger.

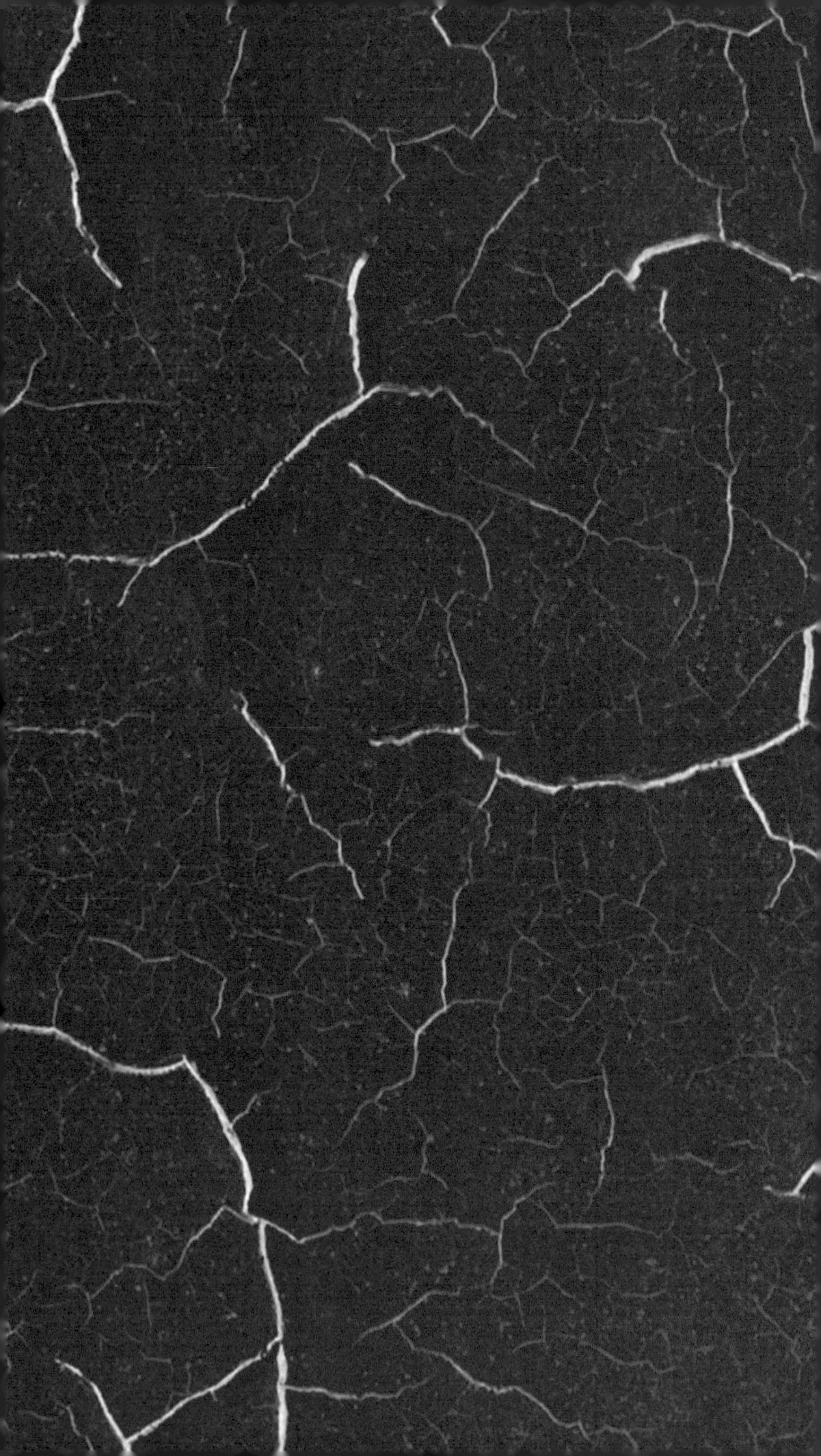

$$5$$

# RAVEN

Then

My first week at work has been so many things. I've stumbled countless times—literally and figuratively. I got orders wrong, I tripped over someone's foot that was sticking out of a booth and fell—while holding a tray of drinks, and I ran to the bathroom to cry when I got yelled at for someone's food being too cold.

It's been harder than I ever imagined. But it hasn't been all bad. In fact, there's a lot that I'm starting to look forward to.

"Payday!" Kyle cheers when checks are handed out in the break room. He holds his up above his head and does a little dance around the room.

I smile at his enthusiasm. I'm just as excited as he is—probably more so.

"Raven, here's yours," Mitch says, handing me an envelope. He smiles. "You've earned it. Good work this week."

My face heats at the praise. "Thank you."

"Not at all," he says. "Thank *you* for being such a great employee."

I bite my lip, smile, then turn to clock in. I'm not sure what it is about Mitch that makes me so—*shy*. It's like all words cease to exist when he's around, or like my brain forgets how to function. I wish I had something more intelligent to say to him, so he would know he didn't hire an idiot.

"Hey, want to hang out after our shift?" Nessa asks as I clock in.

I smile, surprised but glad. She was the hostess the day I came in for my interview, and she's also been one of the most helpful in teaching me the ropes. "I'd love to," I say.

"Great! Some of us from work are getting together at Crystal's—kind of a work get-together thing."

"Oh—okay."

"Is... that okay?"

"Yeah, of course. It's just—I don't really know Crystal. Do you think she'll mind if I'm there?"

Nessa laughs. "Don't even worry about it. Trust me, she doesn't know half the people who sit on her couch. Besides, it's a work thing, like I said." She grins at me. "I'm so excited to hang out with you finally."

I give a weak smile. "Me too." I'm not sure what she means by *finally*—I've only worked here a week. I'm also nervous as hell. *A work thing?* I thought it was going to be just the two of us.

I don't do well with groups of people. I sigh to myself. *I need to make a good impression.* I want everyone here to like me. If I want to keep working here for a while, I'm going to have to do things out of my comfort zone.

WHEN NESSA PULLS UP to the curb outside Crystal's house, I regret agreeing to ride with her. The *work thing* is a full-blown house party. I look at her with wide eyes.

She laughs. "Don't worry, it's fine. Besides, Mitch is even going to be here."

"*Mitch?* Really?"

"Yeah. He and Crystal have a thing I guess." She shrugs.

"It's kinda hard to imagine—"

She laughs. "Trust me, I know!"

We get out of the car and make our way inside, where Nessa leaves me to grab us something to drink. The music is so loud I feel like my head is rattling. I hold myself back from putting my hands over my ears to drown out the sound.

Minutes pass and Nessa doesn't come back, so I decide to walk around and look for her. As I do, I couldn't be more shocked by the variety of everyone's ages. Some are young—so young I wonder if they're even in high school, and some are older—at least in their fifties, maybe even past that.

"Hey, are you lost?" Mitch puts a hand on my shoulder, startling me. He has a drink in his hand and his shirt is untucked. I gape, surprised to see him so relaxed.

"No—sorry, I'm just looking for Nessa."

"She's in the kitchen, I think." He points me in the right direction.

"Thanks." I start to walk away but he stops me.

"Hey, have you met anyone from the other branches?"

"The other what?"

He frowns. "Did Nessa explain what this party is for?"

*I really hope he can't see how red my face is.* "Um—no. She just said Crystal was having a work get-together thing. I didn't really know it was a party."

"I see." He pauses, thinking. "I'm sorry," he says. "I should've expected as much from Nessa."

"So..." I look around at all the people. "All these people work for other branches?"

"Mostly, yes. This party is unofficial—kind of off the books, to celebrate our buying out the *Gary's* chain. That's why it's at Crystals and why I wasn't allowed to personally invite all my employees. We had to rely on word of mouth to get everyone here—and with the alcohol." He shrugs. "I'm not really supposed to be handing that out."

I nod my understanding. It makes sense, I guess. "I'm glad to be a part of it."

Mitch smiles. "Let me show you around."

He leads me around the house, introducing me to people. Some are coworkers at our branch that I haven't met yet, but most are from other branches. Some drove over an hour to get here, which impresses me.

Just as we're in the middle of a conversation, I hear my name. "Raven!" Kyle runs up and grabs me in a bear hug, lifting me clear off the ground. "I wasn't sure if you'd make it!" he cries, setting me back down.

I smile, aware that he's drunk. His carefree nature is so endearing and probably gets him really good tips. "I hitched a ride with Nessa. Have you seen her?"

I notice then how upset Mitch looks. He's almost scowling at Kyle, and I realize how rude we are—totally interrupting the previous conversation. My face heats.

"Yeah, I just saw her. She's over there." Kyle points to a general location in the other room.

I nod my thanks, not bothering to look. I try to ignore him, not wanting to upset Mitch further. I enjoy being his *golden employee* too much, and I'm still too new. Kyle might not have anything to prove, but I sure do.

Mitch clears his throat. "So—like I was saying..." He picks up right where he left off moments ago.

Kyle snickers, giving me a look. He dances away, almost spilling the drink in his hand. As he does, I can't help but notice Mitch watching him from the corner of his eye.

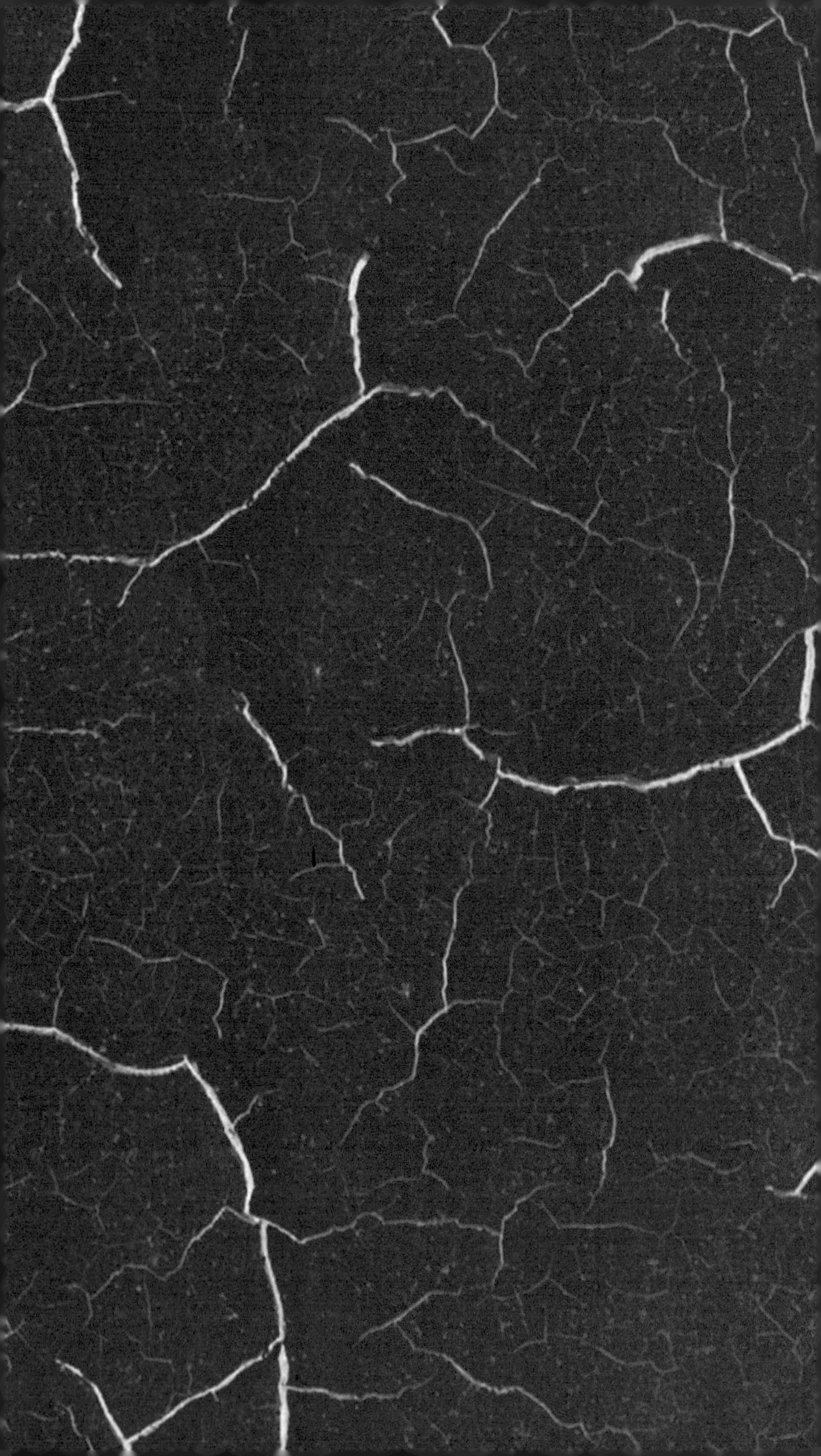

6

———

## MITCH

Now

IF ONE GOOD thing came out of my prison sentence, it's that I'm in the best physical shape of my life. I never thought I'd have a better body now—at forty-five than when I was twenty-five—but here I am. With little else to do during my time there, it quickly became a new way to spend my hours.

I grab the bar on my lat pull-down machine and slowly pull it to my chest. I raise my arms back up over my head, then bring it down again for ten repetitions, relishing the burn. I add more weight, adjust my position, then pull the handle again.

It doesn't take long to build up a sweat. I check my watch, smile, then continue.

An alarm on my watch tells me it's time to move to a new machine. As I stand up, I bump into someone, momentarily blinded by the towel I'm using to wipe my face. "I'm so sorry," I say, trying to help steady the person.

The towel drops from my hands. I take a step back.

Raven and I stare at each other with wide eyes. "M-Mitch?" she croaks.

"It's me." I give a small smile. "How are you?"

"I—" She looks around us. "I'm—what are you doing here?"

"I'm working out... what are you doing here?" I frown. "Are you... you're not following me, are you?"

Raven's jaw drops. "No! I would never."

I sigh. "Good. It's been hard getting back into the groove of things after so long. I just—I'm just trying to get my life back."

She turns scarlet, starts wringing her hands together. "I'm sorry. I didn't mean—" she huffs a breath then looks back up at me with a small smile that lights up her eyes. "It's nice to see you. You look good."

I clench my jaw, trying to maintain my calm. It's a struggle to hold myself back—to not reach for her right here and pull her to me. I nod. "A pleasant surprise bumping into you. Can I—" I shrug. "You wouldn't want to get a cup of coffee after your workout, would you?"

Raven bites her lip, sending blood straight to the part of me that needs it the least. She looks at the watch on her wrist, hesitating. "I shouldn't," she starts.

"Okay, no problem." I hold up my hands, still holding that fake smile to my face, but letting a little hurt show—not too much, just enough to make her feel guilty. "I'll see you around, maybe."

"Wait—" she calls when I take a few steps away.

I turn back toward her, eyebrows raised in question.

"I have someplace to be soon, but I usually grab a smoothie downstairs after my workout. Do you want to meet me in about an hour?"

"Sounds great." My grin is genuine this time. Raven

has always had a problem with worrying too much about other people's feelings. It's a weakness, but also one of the reasons I love her so much. *I always know just how to get her to bend.*

---

AN HOUR LATER, I've rinsed off in the gym shower and am waiting for her by the smoothie shop downstairs. Raven shows up a few minutes later. She clears her throat, unsure of what to say. She smiles up at me, seemingly speechless, and I grin when I see her eyes flick to my biceps.

"Nice workout?" I ask.

She nods. "A little crowded today, but I was able to get my usual machine."

"Oh? Is there something special about it?"

"Not really." Her little laugh sends tingles up my spine. "It just has this little squeak that's so annoying, but I like it because it makes me run a little faster, like I'm trying to get away from it." She shrugs. "Kinda stupid, I know."

"It's not stupid at all. I think that's a brilliant way to push yourself."

She smiles at me, her eyes lighting up her whole face.

We each order a smoothie and take a table by the window. Raven checks her watch again. "I only have a few minutes; I hope you don't mind."

"Not at all. I'm just glad to be able to catch up with you. I tried to write to you a few times."

"Oh—" She fumbles with her words, doesn't know quite what to say. "How long have you... been in town?"

She's embarrassed to ask—curious but doesn't want to seem rude.

"A little while. Not long."

Raven looks like she's trying to do the math in her head. *Yes, it's really been five years.* It probably flew by for her.

"So," I say after a pause. "Tell me about your life."

There are so many things I want to ask her—far more important things. There are so many things I want to tell her too. Like, for starters, how beautiful she is. How I haven't gone five minutes in the last five years without thinking of her. How just the thought of her name makes my heart race. *Soon,* I tell myself. *Soon I'll be able to tell her all the things.*

"There's not much to tell, really," she says, shrugging. "I work at a diner."

"Do you like it?"

"Yes. They're good to me."

"Good. That's good to hear."

She checks her watch again.

"Got to get going?" I ask.

She nods. "I'm sorry, I don't want to be late."

I nod. "No problem, I understand." *Groceries aren't going to buy themselves.*

Raven stands.

I stand with her. "I'll walk you to your car."

She wants to protest but can't think of a reason fast enough, so I follow her lead out the door.

As we walk through the parking lot, I say, "I'd still like to take you out for a cup of coffee. Catch up for real."

She nods absently. "I'd—like that."

"We could exchange numbers so we could set something up. Maybe later in the week you'll be free?"

That same hesitation comes back, making me want to punch something. I hold back. *It's been a long time,* I remind myself. *She's always been a little shy.*

"Sure," Raven finally says. "Good idea." She programs my number into her phone then texts me, so I have hers.

I don't mention anything about her hundred-thousand-dollar car, don't even lift an eyebrow at it. I smile and nod as she waves goodbye then go to get in my own car, making sure she's long gone first.

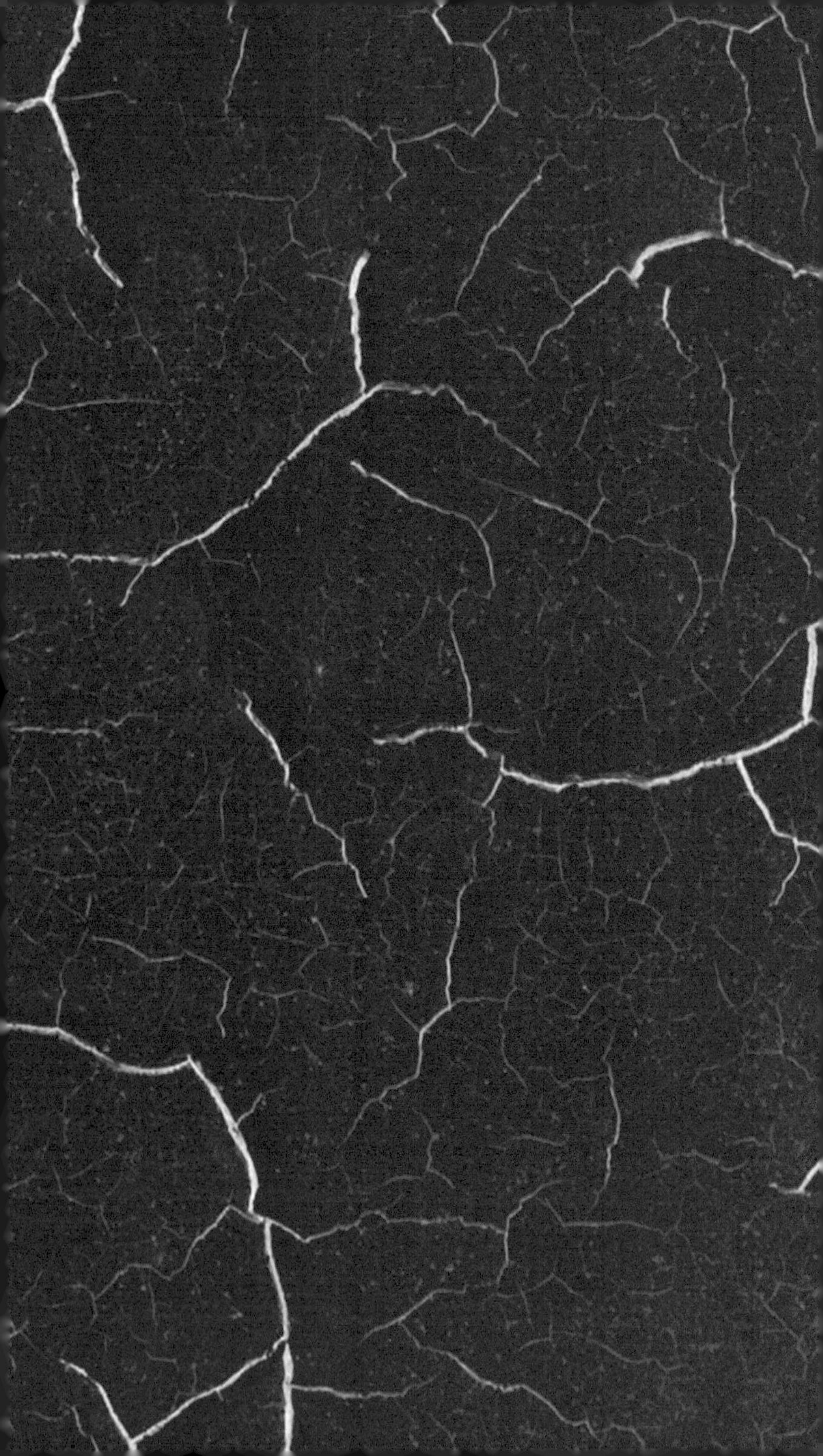

# 7

# THEN

### Raven

A FEW WEEKS after the house party, I notice I haven't seen Kyle around for a while. I don't have a set schedule, it changes every week, so it's not uncommon for me to see different coworkers at varying times. I notice his absence because he's always the happiest on payday. *I wonder if his availability changed.*

I stop by Nessa at her podium. "Have you seen Kyle around?" I ask.

She tilts her head, grinning. "Do you have the hots for him?"

My jaw drops. "What? No. Not at all—"

"Everything okay here, ladies?" Mitch says, approaching.

"Yep. Just fine," Nessa says, winking at me.

Mitch looks at me with a raised brow.

"I was just wondering about Kyle, that's all." My face is on *fire.* I wish he would stop looking at me.

Mitch's lips press together. "Kyle is no longer with us. He quit without notice."

Nessa's eyebrows shoot up, but she stays silent. I do too, too shocked by the news. *I thought Kyle loved it here.*

"Now, if there's nothing else, back to work, please." He continues on, making his rounds. More customers walk in, greeted by Nessa, and I move on to check on my tables.

---

WHEN I LATER SLIP ON my untied shoelaces in the kitchen, Aaron sits with me, letting me cry into his shoulder. "I'm so sorry," I sob. "I don't know what's wrong with me, I'm such a klutz! Mitch is going to fire me."

Aaron pats my back. "Don't worry, when I was a server, I did the same thing. That's why I'm in the kitchen now."

"Really?" I wipe my face and pull back to look at him. "I can't imagine you tripping over anything."

He laughs. "Trust me. Ask Dale if you don't believe me."

Dale has been a server here longer than anyone. If Dale has seen it, then there's no doubt Aaron is telling the truth and not just trying to make me feel better.

I grasp Aaron's hand. "Thank you. And I'm going to do that, you know—ask Dale. I bet he's got some interesting things to say."

He smiles. "You should. You'll get a kick out of it. And you're just getting started. Don't sweat the small stuff so much."

"It's kinda hard..."

We laugh together, then Mitch walks in, his eyes

narrowing at the sight of us. I feel sick to my stomach at the thought of what he must be assuming—the image we present, sitting here on the floor in each other's arms.

I jerk back, distancing from Aaron.

He does the same, stammering. "I—we were just—"

Mitch arches an eyebrow. "This is the second time today I've caught you talking and not working, Raven."

His dry tone sends fear through me. I don't want to lose my job. I look to Aaron. *Is he going to tell Mitch about all the dishes I just broke?*

"She fell," Aaron says. "I was just helping her up."

Mitch's annoyance changes to concern. "Are you hurt?"

"I'm okay. Just had a little shock. I'm sorry. I'll get back to work."

I move to get up and Mitch reaches a hand out to help me. "Aaron," he says. "Let's make sure this doesn't happen again. It's vital that the kitchen is a safe place."

I bite my lip, wanting to defend Aaron, but also not wanting to risk Mitch's disappointment. I watch Aaron for a reaction but he only nods.

"Of course," he says.

I brush myself off and straighten my apron, ready to get back to it. With Kyle quitting, we're back to being short staffed and I know there's no time to waste.

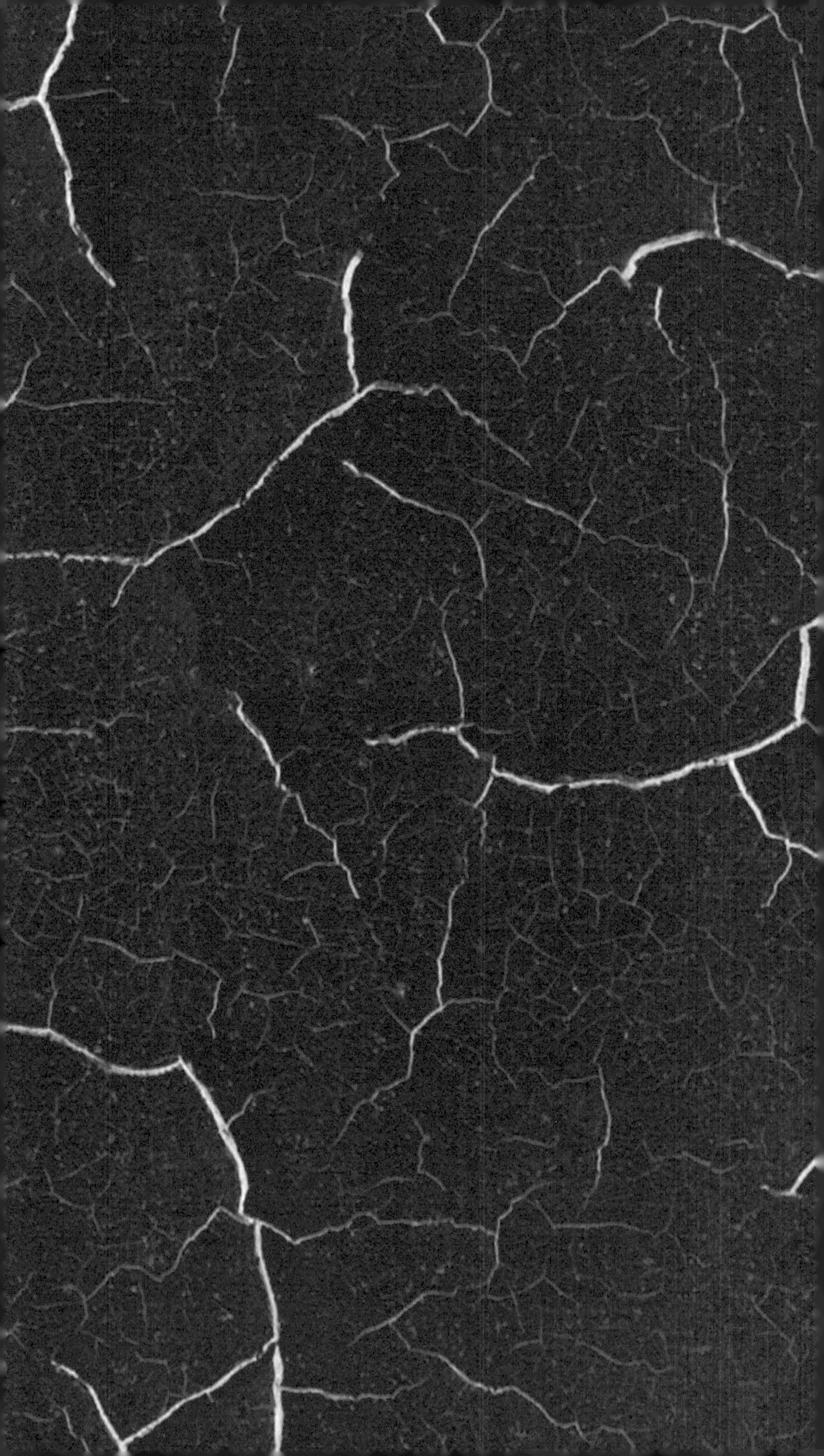

# 8

# RAVEN

Now

"Honey, eggs are ready!" I call to Stephen from the kitchen.

"Okay!" he calls back. "Libby's almost ready."

I smile, wondering what crazy outfit she's going to wear today. Libby has it in her head to put together the fluffiest, brightest, shiniest clothes, full of all the feathers, sequins, and buttons she can find. The more *things* on her, the better. Yesterday, she came out of her room with striped rainbow leggings, a blue feather boa, and a red faux-fur vest over a green polka dot long-sleeve top.

Libby runs to me. "Mom! Daddy won't let me wear this!" She holds up her rainbow leggings under her rainbow sequin shirt that she's wearing. Big crocodile tears stream down her face as she pouts.

I look to Stephen, who's behind her now. "Sorry," he mouths.

"Baby, those pants are dirty. You wore them yesterday, remember?" I say.

"They're clean!"

I point to the peanut butter and jelly stains and offer a smile. "I'll wash them for you today."

"But Mooom!"

"That's it, babe, let's pick out another pair," Stephen says, trying to help.

Libby breaks down into tears again, desperate to get her way.

I check the clock. "Libby, we're going to be late."

"Good!"

"Libby! Honey, what about the furry leggings?" Stephen asks.

I give him a quick look. *Those will be too warm for her today.*

"Or—the polka dot pair?" he rushes to add.

Libby wipes her face. "The furry ones!"

I sigh. *Fine, let her sweat a little.*

---

AFTER A RUSHED BREAKFAST, we're off. Stephen kisses me on the cheek and leaves for work. I take Libby and we're off to her school. "Remember, I'll pick you up this afternoon instead of Daddy," I say before she gets out of the car.

"Okay, Mom. Love you." She kisses me.

I hold her for a minute before she wiggles free. "I love you too!" I call to her as she runs to catch up with her friends. I sigh and get back into the car to head to work.

On the way, I allow myself to think about Mitch. It's the only time I dare to—when I'm alone. I can't even look Stephen in the eye when I think about him, can barely stand to even look at Libby.

*I can't believe it's been five years.* I chew on my lower lip as I navigate traffic. Seeing him at the gym like that—I shake my head. He doesn't *look* like he just got out of prison. I chew harder, drawing blood. *And I really know what someone fresh out of prison looks like, right?*

I honk when someone cuts me off. It takes me about two seconds to speed back around and pull in front of them, right where I was before. *What does he want from me?* I grip the steering wheel harder. *You know what he wants—what he's always wanted.*

*He's not going to get it. Not this time.* I slam on the brakes as I come to a red light. My heart is racing. I feel my pulse in my throat, and it's not from dealing with traffic. *How does he not realize that I'm not interested?*

I clench my jaw. *Maybe he's just being friendly. We just bumped into each other—no. That was no coincidence.* My teeth grind. I turn into the parking lot at work, grimacing both at the taste of blood in my mouth and at how screwed I am.

*Just explain that you have a family now. He'll understand.* I shake my head at the naivete of my inner self. *Mitch always gets what he wants. One way or another.*

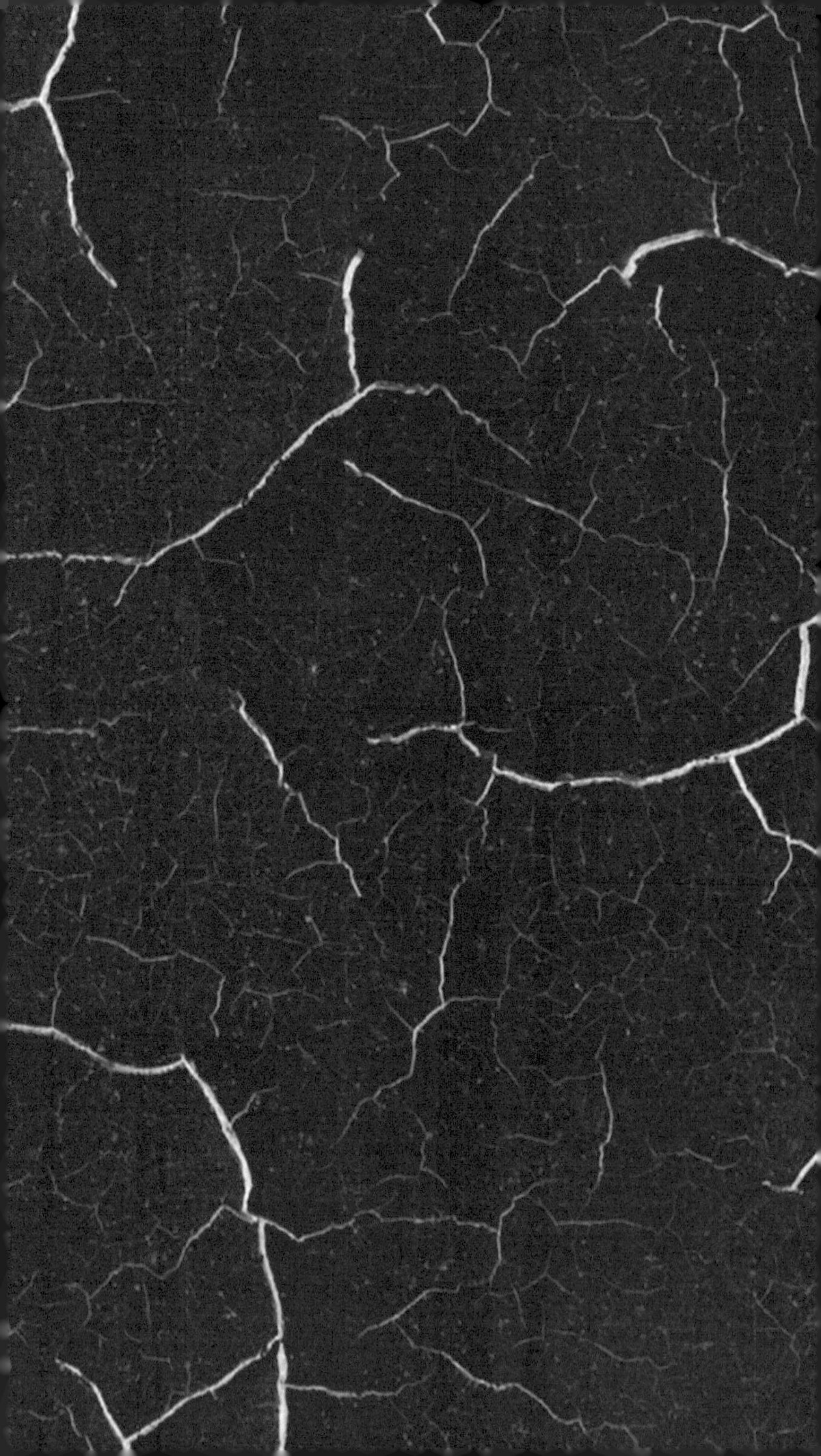

# 9

# RAVEN

Then

I LEAN FORWARD in my seat, checking my watch. *Crap.* I'm going to be late. I haven't been there for six months yet, and already I'm going to be late. I tap my foot, silently urging the bus to go faster.

The lady beside me looks at me sideways. "That's not going to make us get there any sooner."

Blushing, I force myself to stop. "Sorry, just running late."

She gives me an indulgent smile. "We've all been there."

I check my watch again.

The bus pulls up to the bus stop and I rush down the steps. *The American* is only a block away—only a few more minutes. I weigh the idea of running with the idea of showing up a mess. *Mitch would probably rather have me walk in two minutes late.*

Finally outside, I reach for the door handle, but the doors won't open. I check my watch again. *What's going on?* We're supposed to be open for dinner, but the doors are locked.

I peek through the glass, noticing the dim lighting. I tap on the glass. "Hello?"

I look around the sidewalk. *Maybe someone else is waiting to clock in, too.* There's no one else here, though. People walk by, some ignoring me, some staring like I'm trying to rob the place.

I try knocking on the door again. "Mitch?"

A few seconds pass. I'm so worried, I feel my throat tightening, tears threatening to spill. I've never been in a situation like this, and I don't want to get fired for a no-call, no-show.

Finally, there's movement inside. I rap on the door again. "Hello? It's me—Raven."

Mitch comes to the door with a grim expression. He unlocks it for me and lets me in. "Hey, you didn't get the message?" he says.

"No. I—don't have a cell phone," I admit, blushing. "What happened?"

"There's—" He clears his throat. "There's been an accident. We're closed for today. I'm sorry, I hope you'll be okay without the hours."

"Oh—of course. What happened?" Losing six hours will sting a little, but I'll survive. I can't help but wonder what kind of accident happened for them to close the entire restaurant. That has to be a ton of money we're losing.

Mitch frowns. "We lost Aaron."

I suck in a breath. "What do you mean?"

"He was in a wreck. There was a hit-and-run, and his bike—crushed him."

My eyes bulge at the news. *Poor Aaron.* I wipe at the

tears on my cheeks. And he's the chef—which makes sense why they would close down for the night.

Mitch pulls me in for a hug. "I'm sorry, I know you two were close."

I sniff. "He was a good friend. So funny too."

"That he was."

There's a moment of silence before I pull back a little. "I'm sorry. You probably have so much to do. I'll leave."

"Wait." Mitch grabs my hand. "I'll give you a ride home."

"No, you don't have to do that. The next bus will be around soon."

"I'm not going to let you ride the bus home. Not after getting news like this." He squeezes my hand. "Besides, I'm done here for the night."

I nod. "Okay. If you're sure. Thank you."

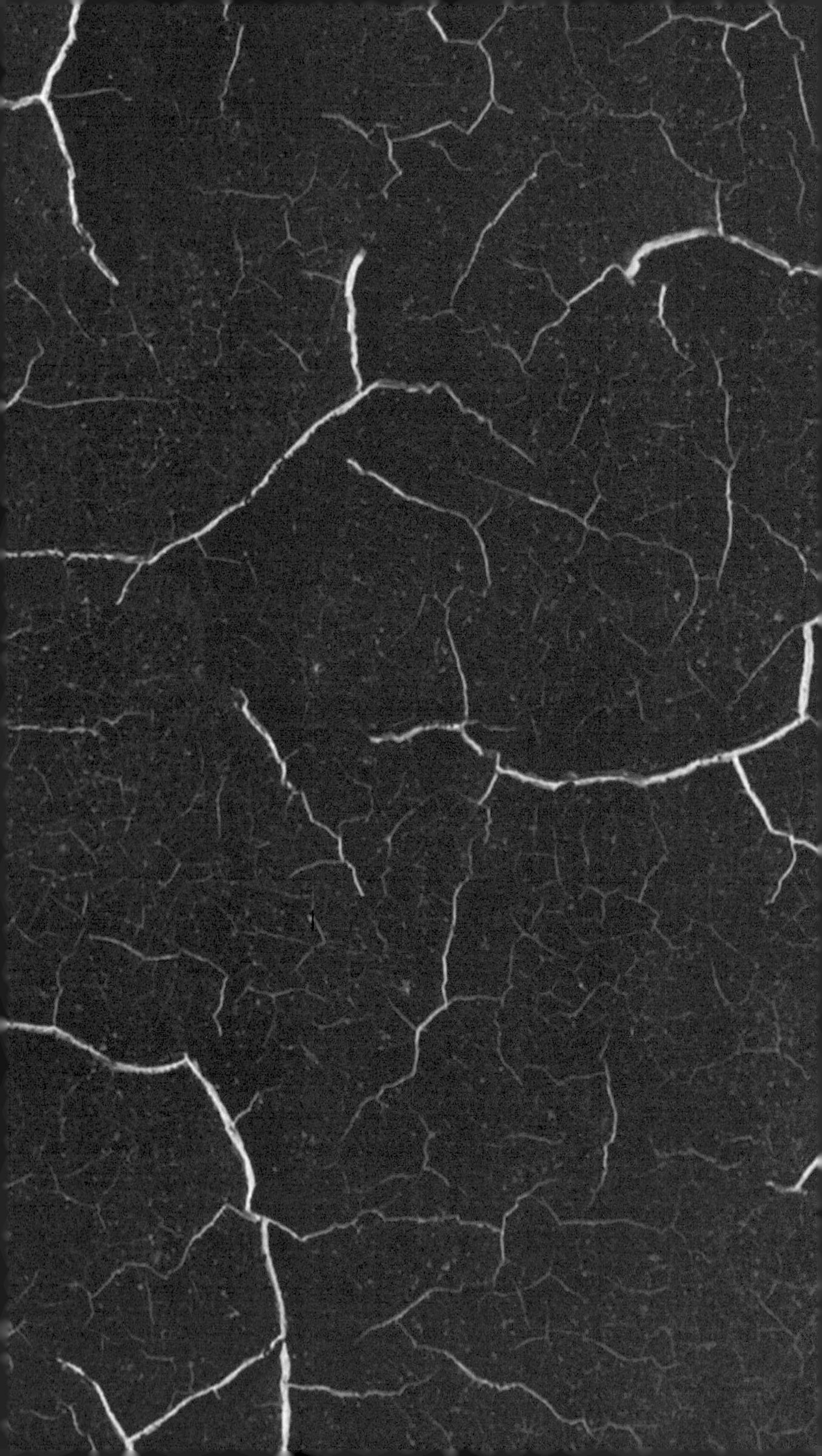

10

---

MITCH

Now

She won't meet my eyes. I find it both endearing and irritating. *What is she hiding?*

"Are you married now?" I ask, nodding to her finger with a diamond the size of a golf ball.

Raven takes a sip of coffee, blushing before answering. "No. We're engaged."

"I see. Congratulations."

"Thanks." She takes another sip.

I knew she would meet me—she's always been incapable of refusing me. I didn't expect her to be so cold toward me though. *It never used to be like this.* She was always so eager to please. I'm trying to keep my patience with her—it's been five years after all.

"Do you—" I clear my throat. "Do you have any kids?"

She bites the inside of her cheek, then shakes her head. "No."

I frown but nod. *Why is she lying?* I drink from my

own coffee as we sit in stilted silence. I fight the urge to grind my teeth. *It never used to be like this.*

"Tell me about your man. What's his name?"

Raven finally meets my gaze. "He's a good man, Mitch."

"I'm glad to hear that. What's his name?"

"Stephen."

"How'd you meet?"

"Why don't we talk about something else? What have you been up to since you've been out?"

I can't help but smile. "I've been doing this and that." *Watching you.* "It's hard to start over." I shrug.

She frowns. "Are you in touch with any of the others?"

*Yes.* "No. Are you?"

"No."

*Liar.* "Can we talk about—before?"

Raven's face goes red. She fumbles for words. "We—no—we don't have to."

"I want to though."

"Really it—we—"

"I wanted to apologize."

Her eyes are saucers.

"If I ever made you uncomfortable, I didn't mean to." I let out a deep sigh. "I'm so sorry, Raven."

Her throat bobs. She nods, unable to speak.

"I've had a lot of time to think, and the one thought plaguing me is that I hurt you. I—I should've known better. I don't expect forgiveness. I know it's too late for that. But—I just hope there can be a future for us still."

Raven's mouth drops. "I—Mitch—I'm with Stephen."

"I know, I know. I meant, just as old friends." I shrug

again. "You're the only one I know around here, the only one I've met so far, and it's been—kind of lonely."

The best way to get Raven to do what I want her to do is to play off her emotions. It's worked from day one and continues to work now. She's always been a creature of sympathy, always too worried about hurting *feelings*.

"Okay," she says. "The past is the past. Let's let it go."

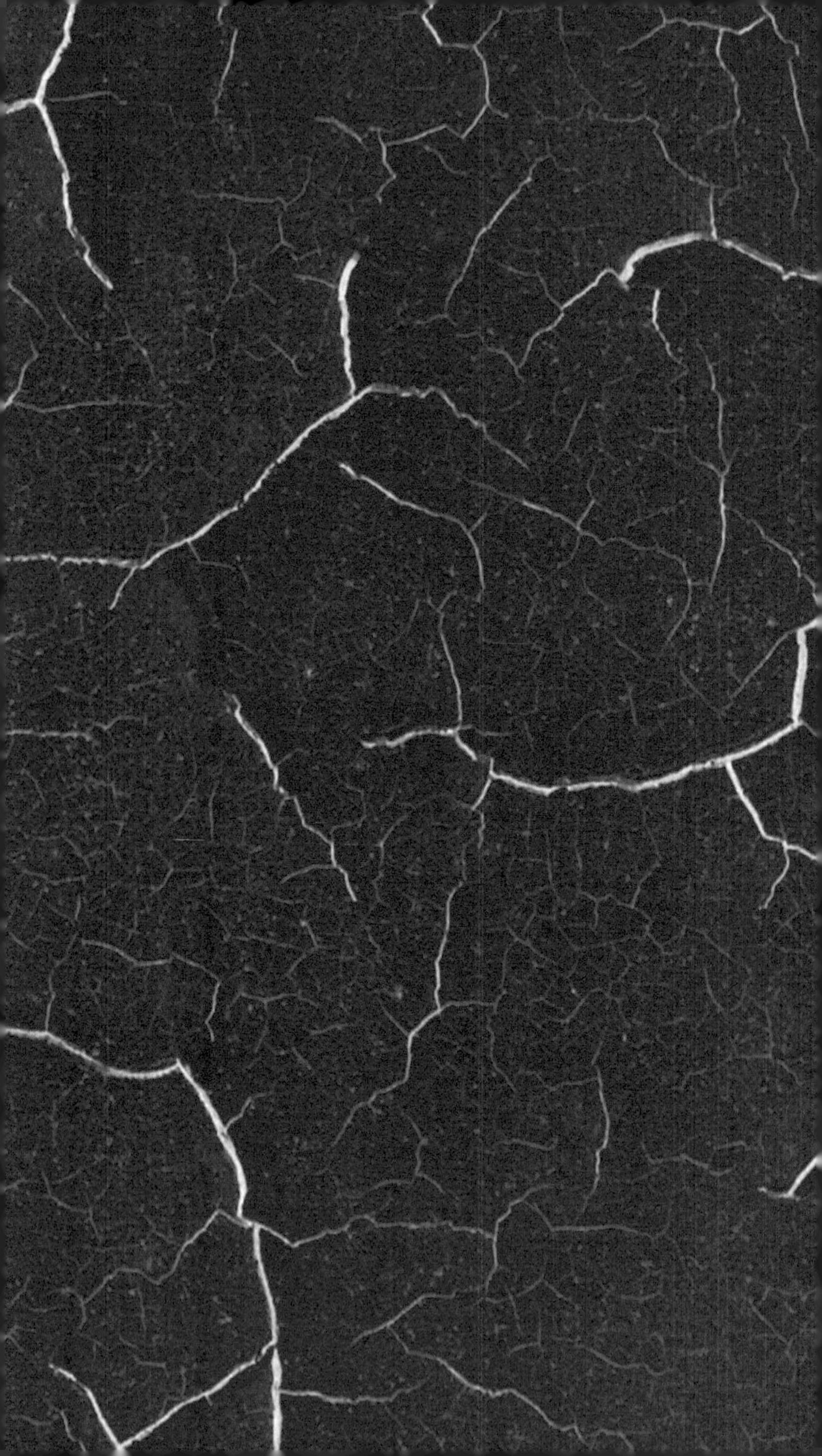

11

## MITCH

Then

Tonight is insane. We're still struggling with our kitchen staff after Aaron's accident, and Nessa decided to call out, along with one of the servers. We're understaffed, to say the least, and to top it all off, it's a Saturday. Customers are lined up around the corner, waiting for tables and those already seated are starting to tap their legs with the anxious desire to be fed.

I've been running around, helping staff in all areas as much as I can. Everyone is tired and needs a break. This isn't the first time we've been in this situation, and it won't be the last. *It's better than not having anyone walk through the door,* I remind myself.

"Hey Mitch, there's someone up front who wants to speak with a manager," Raven says, carrying a tray of drinks past.

"Hang on a second," I call. She stops and turns to me, flushed.

I can't help but smile. *She's one of the hardest workers here.* "You're doing a great job today."

She beams. "Thanks."

"Don't overextend yourself, okay? I know we're busy but give yourself a breather."

Raven nods. "Okay. I won't—I mean, I will." Her flush grows deeper.

I nod to her, pat her on the shoulder and we each continue on our way. As I'm listening to an angry patron complain about how long he and his family have had to wait to be seated, the only thought getting through is *Raven.* The way she smiles at people, the way she's so eager to please everyone, the way she carries herself.

The road I'm going down is a dangerous one. It's unprofessional, inappropriate, *crazy.* I'm helpless to resist, though. There's something about her that draws me in, despite all the logic in the world, all the reasoning.

---

THROUGH THE WINDOWS, I see the sunset slowly fade into the night. The darker it gets, the hungrier the people are. Business isn't letting up, not yet. I glance at my watch and cringe. Raven is supposed to be off soon.

I find her in the kitchen, grabbing some plates of food. "Hey, I have a big favor to ask," I say.

"Sure, anything."

The words, and her look, make my heart race. "Will you stay until closing tonight? Or at least until it slows down? I know you're supposed to be off soon, but without you here it's going to be a nightmare."

Raven bites the inside of her lip. She knows she needs to go home, but she also doesn't want to let me or anyone else down. "Okay," she finally says. "I'll need a ride home later, if that's okay?" She blushes, embarrassed to ask.

"Of course, it's no problem. And you are an absolute angel! Thank you, I mean it." I stare into her eyes, so she knows how sincere I am.

Her blush grows deeper. She smiles at the praise and nods. "I'm glad to help. I'll just call home and let them know I'll be late."

"Excellent." I leave her to step into my office. My heart rate hasn't slowed down yet. I look down at my damp palms and shake my head. *Get it together, Mitch.*

IT'S FINALLY SLOWED DOWN ENOUGH for me to take Raven home. She climbs into my truck, and I close the door for her before getting in to start the ignition. As we drive, she leans her head against the window and sighs.

"I bet you're exhausted," I say. "Thanks so much for staying. You have no idea how much it meant."

"I'm glad to help. We were so busy tonight." She bends forward a little to massage her calves. She twists her ankles in circles, doing small stretches with her feet.

"You can take your shoes off if you want."

"That's okay."

She wants to though. I can see how her fingers itch to massage her sore feet. She's too embarrassed to take me up on the offer.

"I don't mind, really. And if you stink us up, we can just roll down the window." I grin at her, trying to release some of her tension.

It works because she laughs and then slips off the

shoes. A moan escapes her lips as she rubs her tender feet in slow circles. She works one foot at a time in slow, deep movements, closing her eyes as she does.

I clear my throat and try to keep my eyes on the road. *You're going to get in a goddamn accident if you keep staring at her!*

Raven is too distracted to notice we should've been to her house by now. When we're stopped and the engine is off, she starts to open the door, thinking we're in her drive-way. But we're not.

Her jaw drops. She turns to me. "Where are we?"

"Beautiful, isn't it?"

"Yes—but—"

"I know, I'm sorry. I should've asked but I wanted to show you this place and I wanted it to be a surprise. I hope that's okay?"

We're parked on a ledge in a forested area, over-looking a river. The full moon lights up the water below. I roll down my window so she can hear the sounds of the night—an owl hooting, the rushing water, critters moving through the brambles.

"It's so peaceful," she says.

"This is where I come to think sometimes."

Before I lose my nerve, I reach a hand across the bench seat to hold hers. She startles and gasps. "Mitch—"

"I have to tell you, Raven, how much I've come to care for you. I know it's inappropriate, I just can't hold it in anymore. You—are simply amazing."

Her eyes are huge. She looks nervous, scared, but at the same time, something more. Maybe—excited? She's thinking, hasn't responded yet, so I push on.

"You're all I think about day and night. I don't want to make you uncomfortable—that's the last thing I ever want. I just have to know if there's a chance you might feel the same?" I shake my head. "No—I know you don't. Couldn't possibly—"

To my immense surprise and satisfaction, Raven grips my hand harder. "It's okay," she says with a weak smile. "I like you too."

I reach across to kiss her. She allows it, doesn't push me away. At first, she doesn't respond—is almost frozen, but slowly she warms toward me.

When she shows no signs of discomfort, no signs that I should stop, I reach my other hand to touch her thigh and slowly, gently, move it upward. She gasps, surprised at my bold move. "It'll be our little secret," I whisper in her ear.

She's silent as we make love. When we're done, I drop her off at home, where her mom waits for her on the front porch.

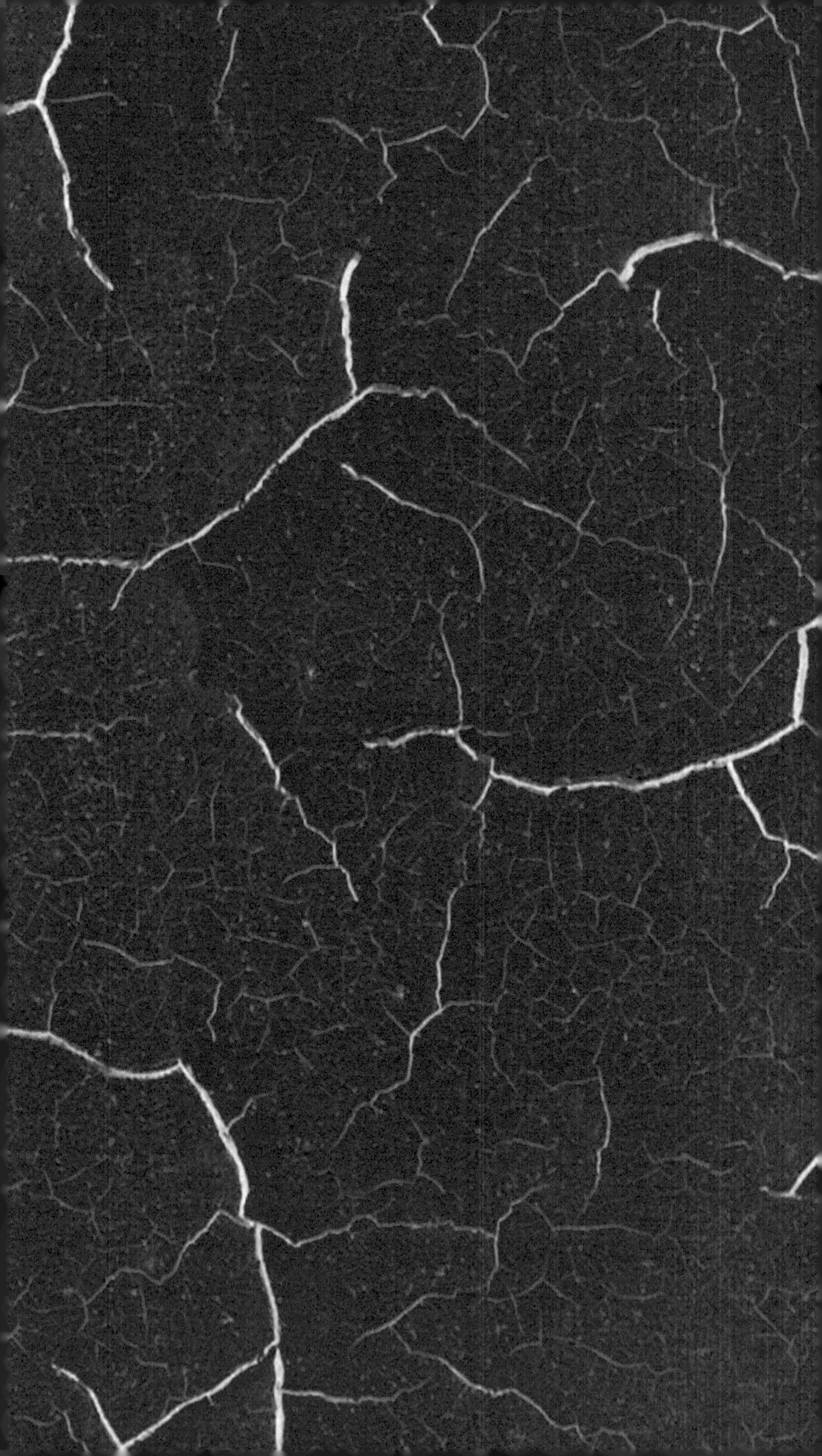

# MITCH

Now

My funding is limited, therefore my options are limited. I'm forced to get creative. What do rich guys do for fun? *Golf.*

It's not hard. I used to be financially set, *before*. I know how to blend in, and with minimal effort, I find myself on the golf course.

*Stephen* and his friend are just ahead of me. I can't help but stare. I analyze all his features—his height, build, *age*. My jaw clenches. *Is that the kind of man Raven wants? Nice and young?*

He's got a decent swing, I'll give him that much. I watch him drive the ball and finish with a birdie. He cheers, pleasantly surprised. His friend is a good sport about it for the most part, but there is a little good-natured annoyance in his tone.

Lucky for me, the course is tight, and the holes are close enough together to give me exactly what I need. I line up my ball and take aim. I swing, make the hit, and watch it fly with a satisfied smile. "Fore!" I cry, running.

Stephen and his friend instantly duck and cover. The ball smacks into their golf cart, just above Stephen's head. *Damn good shot, Mitch.*

"I'm so sorry," I yell, still running toward them.

They both stand back up. "No harm done," Stephen says. His eyes crinkle in the corners when he smiles, making me want to punch him.

"I hate to be rude," I say. "But would you two mind if I joined you? I'm playing solo and could use a little friendly competition if I wouldn't be imposing."

They look at each other then both shrug. The friend says, "Sure, we'd love to have you." He extends a hand. "I'm Jack. This is Stephen."

"Good to meet you both. I'm Mitch." I shake with each of them, then we move to play.

---

WHEN THE LAST shot is finally made, I feel like I could pull my hair out. I've had about all I can take of these gentlemen but sadly, I'm not through yet. "How about that nineteenth hole?" I ask with a grin.

Jack and Stephen both nod, smiling. "I'm up for a victory celebration," Stephen says.

*I bet you are.*

"First drink's on me," Jack says.

We meet at the clubhouse bar and toast to a good round. When our drinks are drained, Jack goes to order us more. "I better not," I say with a sheepish smile. "Wouldn't want to upset the wife."

Jack grimaces. "Sounds about like Stephen's situation."

Stephen laughs. "Raven doesn't mind if I drink. I just don't want to go home drunk to her. I might not be able to perform my husbandly duties." He wiggles his eyebrows.

My fists clench at his words and even harder at the look on his face. *You aren't her husband yet, asshole.* I try not to grind my teeth as I imagine him touching her. Instead, I smile. "Exactly my point. You're not married, Jack?"

He shakes his head. "No, thank God."

Stephen and I laugh. By now, we're all on a friendly level. I've earned their trust.

"How often do you play?" Stephen asks.

"Not as much as I'd like. It's hard with the baby. I like to be home to help out as much as I can."

Stephen nods. "I know what you mean. My daughter is a handful sometimes."

My eyebrows arch as I nod my understanding. "How old?"

"Five—going on twenty-five."

We laugh and Jack gives a disgusted look. "And this is exactly what I don't want to have to deal with."

"I've got news, my friend. Not marrying doesn't prevent kids," Stephen says, still laughing.

"Yeah, and I might not even have to sleep with her to wind up with one," Jack quips under his breath.

Stephen sucks in a breath, stares at Jack with wide eyes. I hold my own—unable to believe what I've just heard. No, there has to be some kind of mistake.

"I think we've had enough," Stephen says, standing. He extends his hand to shake with me. "Let me give you my number. You can call me the next time you're up for a round."

We exchange information and Stephen goes to leave, only nodding in Jack's direction. I extend a hand toward Jack. "It's been a pleasure."

He gives me a grim smile. "Likewise. I'd love to play another round, anytime." He gives me his phone number too, and I walk away with a racing heart full of hope and satisfaction.

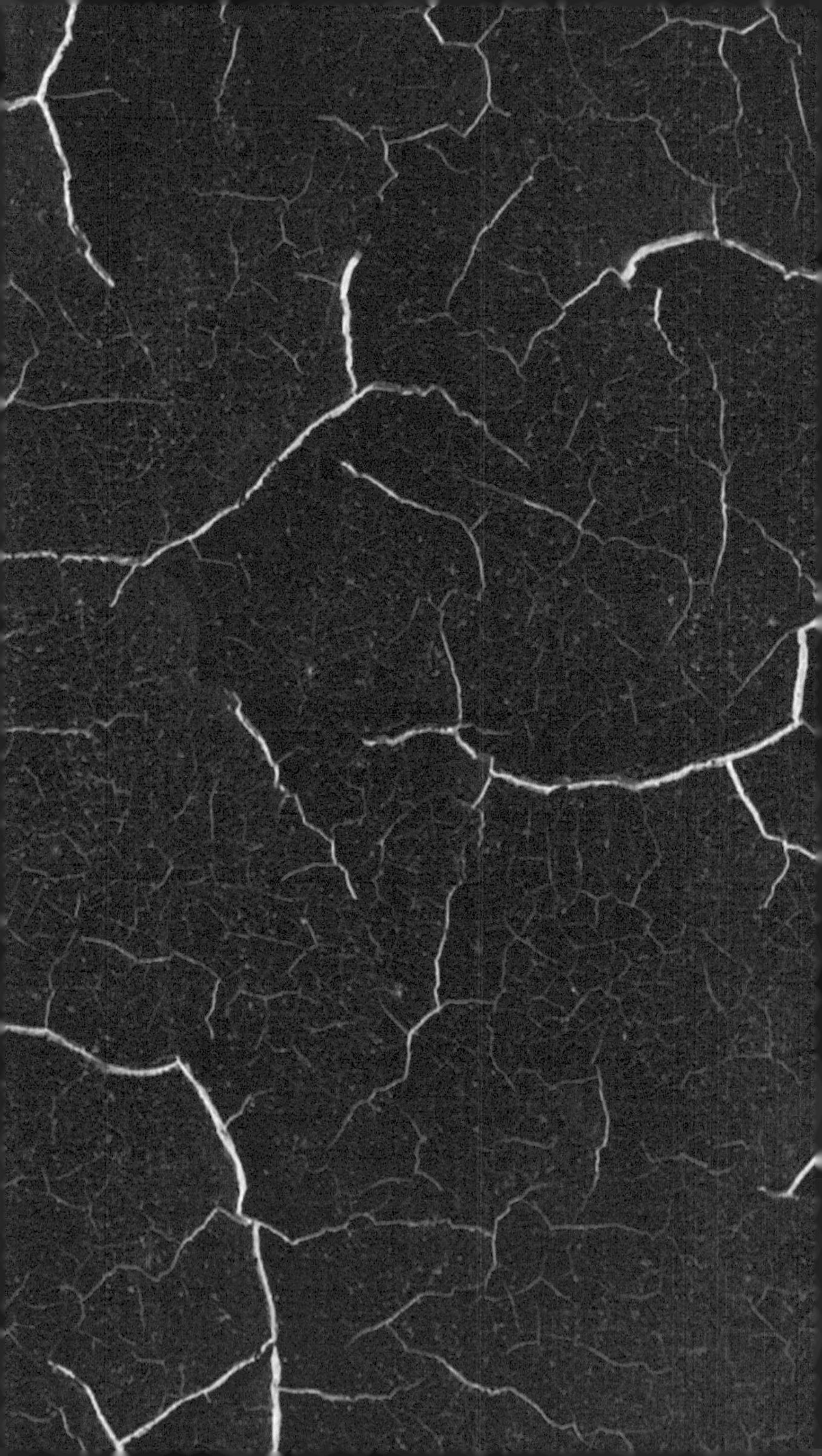

13

———

RAVEN

Then

I FEEL so... weird. It's like there's something written on my face that's invisible to me but clear to everyone else. At school, I feel so naked—like everyone's eyes are on me and won't stop staring.

I keep my head down all day, my eyes glued to my shoes. It's my usual behavior, for the most part. My best friend, Devin, is the only one who mentions anything.

"Hey, how was your weekend?" he asks.

"Fine."

"Fine good or fine bad?"

"Fine fine. Just fine." I'm on edge, like there's something crawling up my skin and I can't help but snap at him. This feeling—I feel like someone else, like I'm out of my own body and inside of someone else's.

"Jeez, sorry," Devin says, taking a step away.

"I'm sorry, I'm just not feeling that great."

He shrugs. "It's okay." But I know it's not. We don't

snap at each other, and we don't argue. Ever. It's why we get along so well.

I give him a quick hug. "I'll see you after class." I leave him in the hallway and head to biology.

---

THE LESSON TODAY is on plant reproduction. I try not to cringe at every word my teacher says but it's a struggle. My jaw is clamped down, my teeth grinding, as I squirm in my seat and try to focus on something else—anything else.

"Raven?"

I flinch when my teacher calls on me. *God, why today?* I turn to him with wide, innocent eyes. "Yes?"

"Would you like to answer?"

I didn't hear the question, but I can't admit that and I struggle with what to say.

Someone across the room snickers. "Don't talk so much, *Raven*."

My teacher didn't hear the comment. "Next time, pay attention," he says with a frown.

I blush and nod and somehow manage to not throw up for the rest of class. Every few minutes I force myself to nod along with what he's saying at the front of the class, force myself to make eye contact to *show* I'm paying attention. When the bell rings, I stand to blend in with everyone else.

"Raven, hang on."

I sigh inwardly and stop at the front of the room. He touches my shoulder and I flinch without thinking.

"Is everything okay?" He takes his hand back, eyeing me with concern.

"Yeah. Just had a long weekend."

"If there's anything you need to talk about, my door is always open."

"Thanks, Mr. Gomez. I'm fine, promise." I paste a fake smile on my face before heading out the door.

I hide in the bathroom when the bell rings again. I'm supposed to be in English, but I can't sit through it again. We're discussing *Romeo and Juliet* today—just the thought makes me nauseous.

When the halls are silent, everyone in their classes, moving on with the day, I stand in front of the mirror. I stare at myself, wondering, *What does everyone see?*

I tilt my head this way and that, bending forward across the sink to get a closer look. Nothing out of the ordinary. *Then why do I feel so hollowed out?*

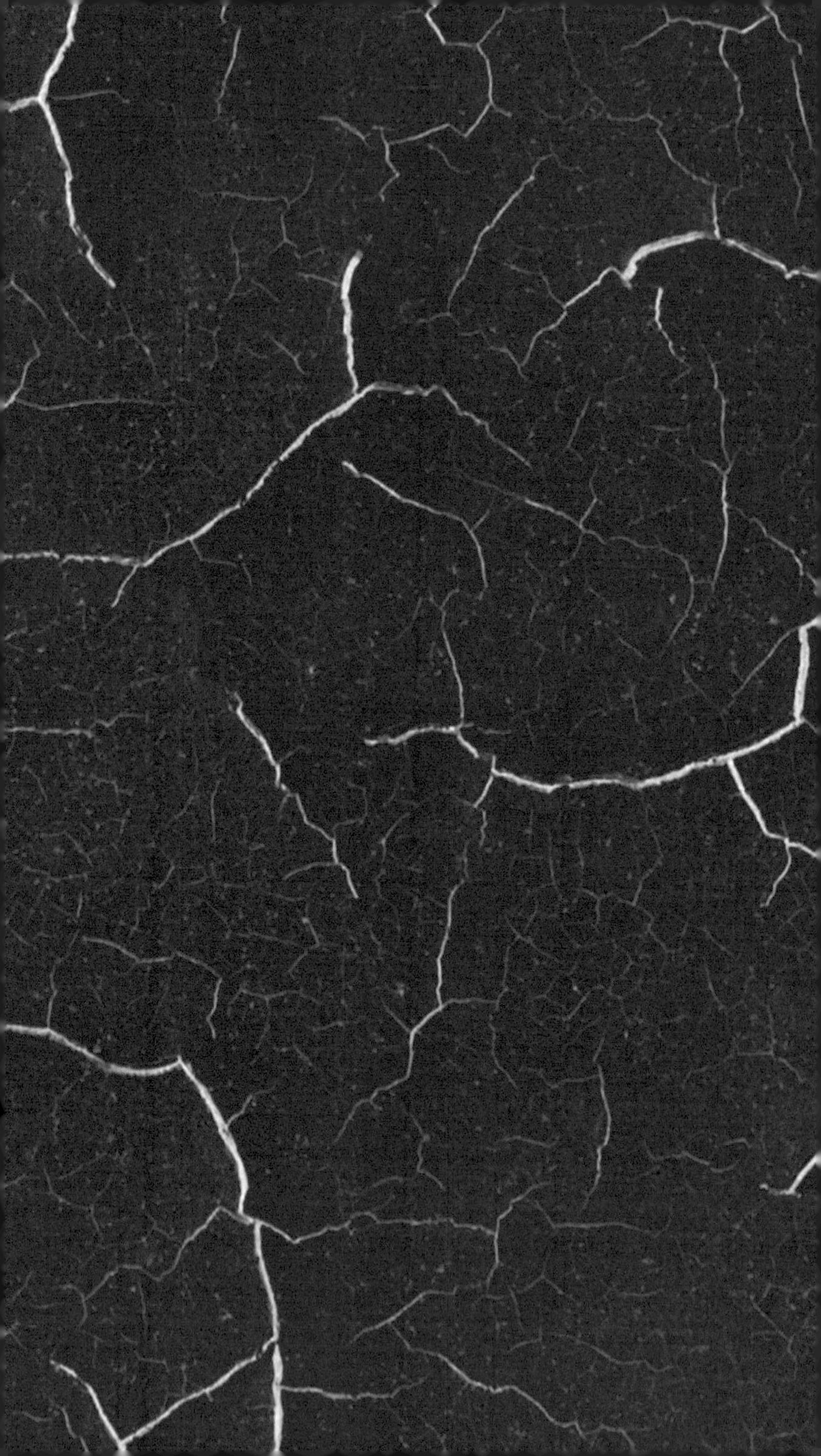

# 14

## MITCH

Now

"So, how did you two meet?" I ask before Jack swings his driver. This is our second meeting and already it's like we're old pals.

"Funny story, actually," he says. "We met through work but weren't really friends. I was about to get fired, believe it or not, but Stephen talked our boss into giving me another chance."

I laugh. "Funny how things work out."

"Isn't that the truth?"

We get in the golf cart and head down the course to the balls. We each switch to an iron. "Too bad he couldn't play today," I say.

"Oh yeah." Jack waves a hand, readying himself to swing again. "Sometimes Stephen lets work get the better of him." He looks around and whispers conspiratorially, "Sometimes, he's even late to pick up their kid because he's *that* into it."

I raise my eyebrows. "I bet his wife isn't happy about that."

He scoffs. "She isn't really his wife. And—" He looks around again, and whispers, "I'm not sure the kid is his either."

"Oh..."

"I mean—" he sighs. "It doesn't really matter. Who am I to judge? It's just there's something about her—his *wife* that is, that I don't like. She seems—I don't know, off somehow."

"What do you mean, off?" I take my swing.

"Hey, nice shot!" Jack says. "I don't know what I mean really. She won't let anyone touch her, won't even shake hands. She's got—shifty eyes. I guess there's something about her that just rubs me the wrong way."

"So that makes you think she's lying about their kid?"

"Honestly, yeah. I think she's got a shady past or something."

I frown. I try not to but can't help my reaction to this idiot. He doesn't even know what he's saying, and anyone who doesn't like Raven doesn't know what they're missing out on. I can't help but want to defend her.

"So... how do you know he's forgotten to pick up the kid?"

"Didn't say that." Jack switches to his putter. "I said, he's been late. And quite a few times, from what I understand."

"He tells you?"

Jack laughs. "Oh yeah. He's asked me to pick her up for him. I've done it too—damn my tender heart."

"Is that weird? The school just lets you?"

"Oh yeah, they're a small establishment. I just give them my name since I'm on the 'okay' list."

"Wow, lucky for them you're able to help."

"That's for sure." He makes his final swing and says, "Par."

"So, you must live close to Stephen then?"

Jack looks at me like he's seeing me for the first time. His eyebrows shoot up. "Not close... no."

I shrug. "I was just thinking with you picking up the kid—"

He tilts his head. "Eh, it's only occasionally. Emergencies, really. I like to complain, that's all. It's really no biggie."

I make par and we get ready to move to the next tee. "I feel like a teenage girl gossiping about Stephen like this," Jack finally says. "Let's talk about something else. Tell me about yourself."

I smile to myself and tell him all about my imaginary wife and child.

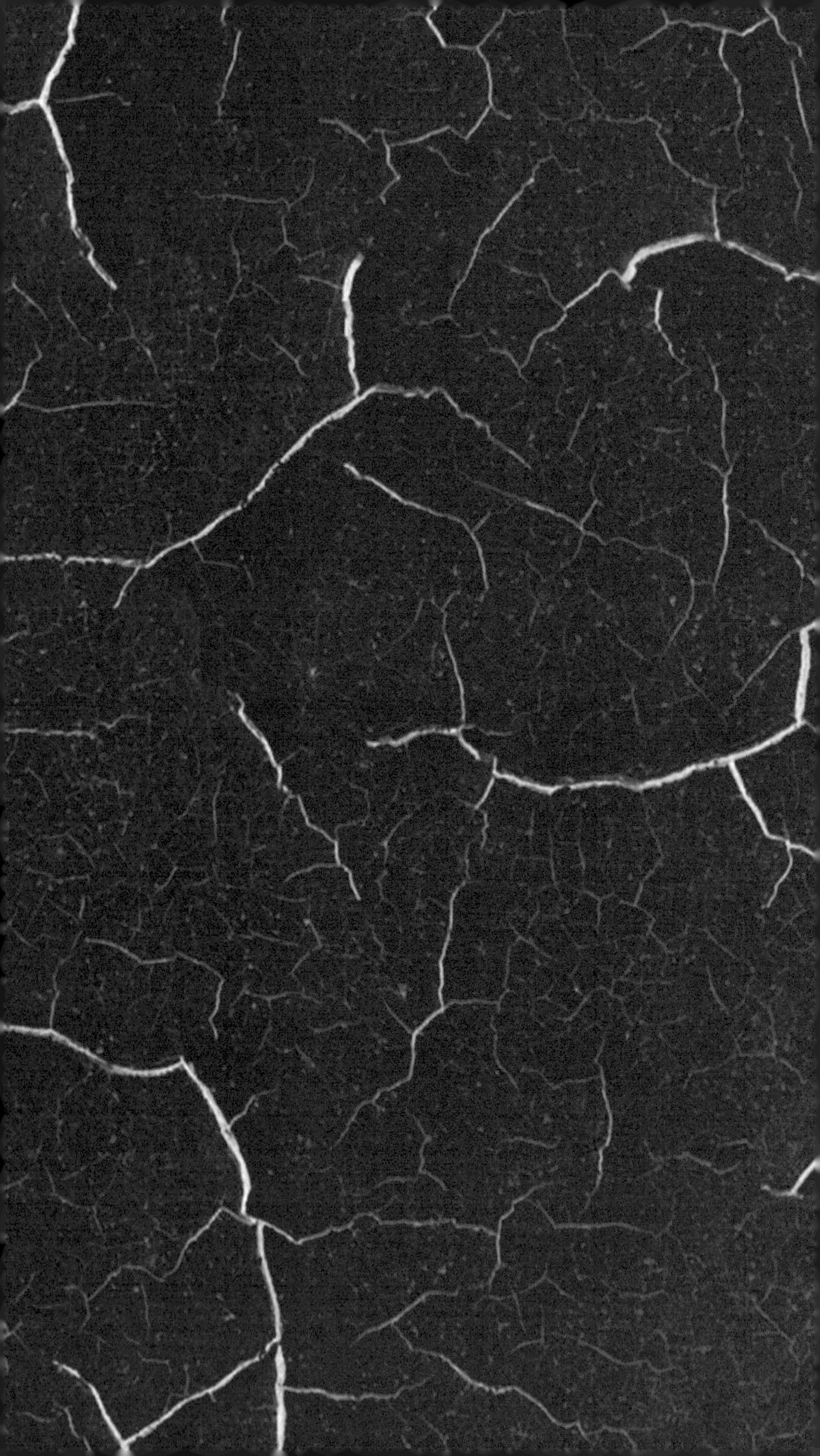

# 15

## RAVEN

*Then*

CALLING into work has never crossed my mind. Until now. As I get ready, I constantly have to wipe my palms against my clothes to dry them off.

My shirt is so sweat stained when I've only been in it five minutes, I have to change into another. My fingers shake as I pull up my pants zipper. The fabric catches and I struggle to get it free without ripping.

*Get a grip already! He didn't hurt you.*

My face is on fire. I try not to think about what he—what *we* did. *It doesn't matter. It was nothing.*

There's no way I can call out sick. He would think there was something wrong and there's *not*. I don't want to call attention to myself. I can't let whatever this is affect my job. I love my job, I love working, and nothing is going to get in the way of that.

THE BUS IS TOO crowded today. "Can I sit here?" someone asks, pulling my mind out of the fog.

I look around. Frowning when I see there are no other seats available. I don't want to be a jerk, so I move my bag out of the way. "Sure, I guess."

I don't even get a smile in return. I try to keep my face pointed out the window but the entire time it's hard for me to breathe. I feel like I'm constantly gasping for breath.

My leg keeps jerking on its own. I scratch all over and squirm in my seat. *He's not even touching me!*

"Hey, are you okay?" the guy asks.

"Fine," I ground out.

I squeeze my eyes shut and keep my head toward the window. *One... two... three... four...* the seconds tick by so *slow!* I take another deep breath, remind myself that I'm not trapped, I can get up and get off the bus any time I want.

*He's too close, he's too close.*

*I can stop it any time I want.*

My eyes fly open. "I need to get up."

The man next to me looks confused. "Uh, sure. I'll let you out when we stop."

"Now!" I yell at him, and the entire bus goes silent. My face flames and my mouth falls open at the look on the man's face. "I'm sorry," I say. "I'm not feeling well. I'm sorry."

He stands to let me out without speaking, his expression says enough.

I make my way to the front of the bus as the driver slows to let me off. My face crumples in on itself as I try to keep from crying. *I am not going to fall apart!*

The driver closes the doors behind me. Within moments the bus is gone and I'm alone. I've never been this nervous to go to work, not even on my first day. *There's nothing to be nervous about*, I remind myself.

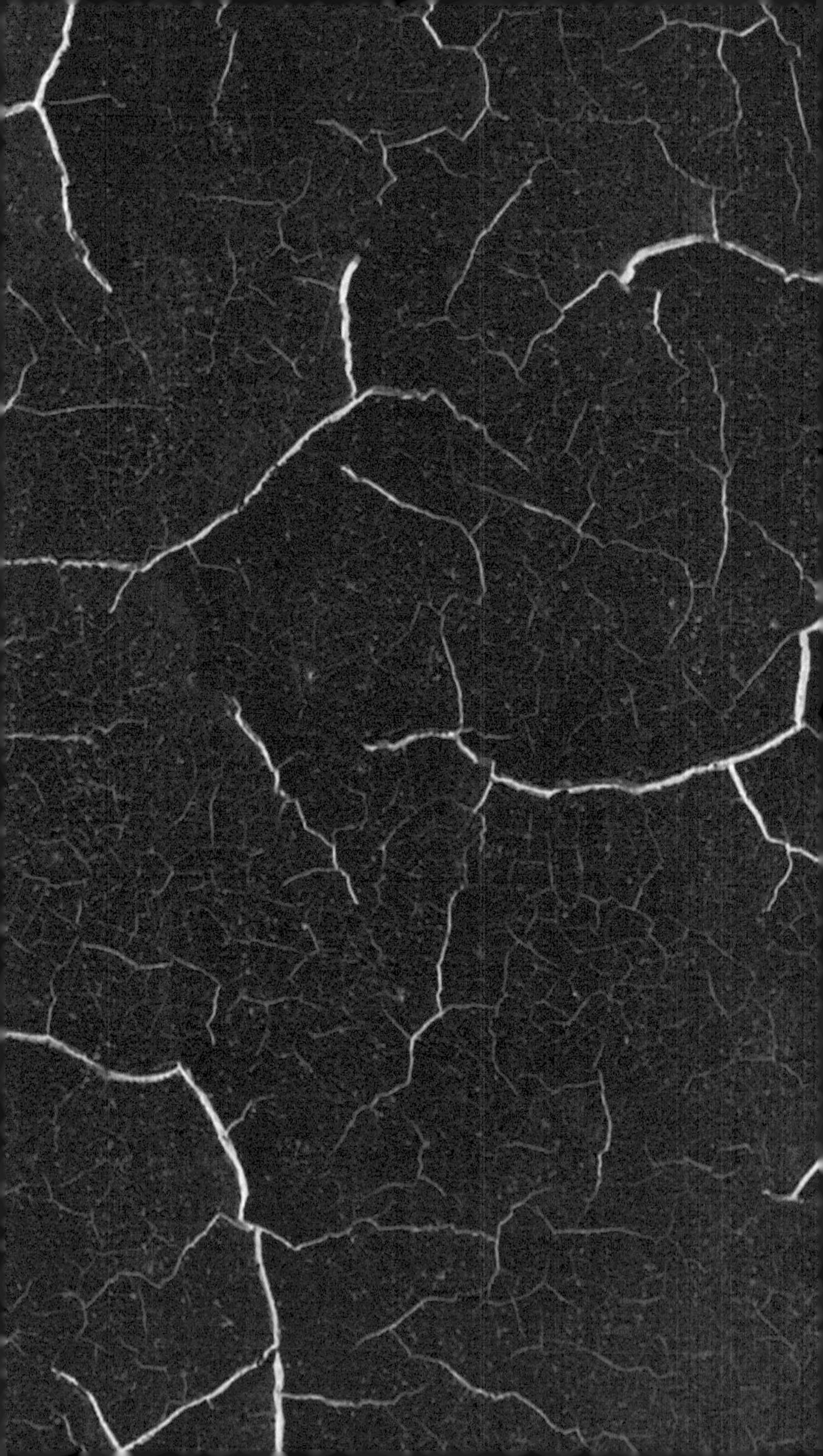

# 16

## RAVEN

Now

WE ALL SLEPT in this morning. I reach my arm across to silence my alarm for the third time and notice the time. My eyes widen as adrenaline wakes me up the rest of the way. "Stephen, wake up. We have to go!"

I give his arm a little shake. He stops snoring but still isn't fully awake. "What?" he mumbles, still half-asleep.

"We're late!" I cry, fumbling with the blankets that are wrapped around my legs. The more I pull, the more tangled they become, until I finally give up and yank them all off the bed.

"Hey!" Stephen yells, his skin prickling with goose-flesh at the sudden loss of warmth.

"Sorry! I have to get Libby. God, we're never gonna make it out of here on time."

"What time is it?" he calls as I move into the bathroom.

I don't bother answering. There's no time. Stephen is definitely not a morning person, but I can't help being a little irritated with him for staying out with his friends the night before... even if it was a "work thing."

When he's out late, I'm up late with Libby because she can't stop worrying about where her daddy is. If he's not there to tuck her in at night, she stays awake until he comes through the front door, then passes out in our bed. No matter what I try, or how I beg and plead with her, it's how it goes every time.

Stephen does so much for us, and he's such a good dad. It's not fair for me to ask him to give up his social life completely. But when we're running late—I can still hold my own little grudge, even if it is misplaced.

When I come back from the bathroom and Stephen is still in bed, I call, "Your meeting is in half an hour!" It finally gets him going.

We scramble to get ourselves and Libby ready and out of the house, knowing we're already off to a rough start. I kiss each of them before handing over a granola bar and piece of fruit for the car ride. "You're still picking up today, right?" I ask Stephen as they get into his car.

He waves to me. "Yes. Have a good day!"

I sigh with relief, then climb into my own car. I text Crystal at work, knowing she'll cover for me. "So sorry! Going to be a few minutes late!"

My phone vibrates as her response comes through, already on my way to the diner. "No prob. Drive safe."

EVERYTHING IS GOING WRONG TODAY, it seems. Work is crap. Crystal is nowhere to be seen when I come in late. Apparently, she *forgot* to let our boss know I texted. I want to kick myself. *I should've known better.*

"I'm sorry, Janna," I say when she gives me that disappointed look that I hate. "I know you don't have your phone on you, and I just thought Crystal would cover for me for a few minutes. I'll know better next time."

"Crystal isn't even here today," Janna says.

My eyebrows furrow. "I texted her—she never said—"

Janna huffs. "She left a few minutes ago, throwing up, sick as a dog. It's fine. Just next time, don't rely on her, okay?"

"Yeah, definitely. I'm so sorry."

Janna rushes to serve waiting customers, while I make my way to the kitchen to see what I can do to help get us caught up. With me being late and Crystal being gone, we're backed up with orders and busier than usual.

When business finally slows, I text Crystal, "Hope you're feeling better." I feel closer to her than any of my other coworkers, considering our past.

"Thanks," she responds. "Sorry to bail on you."

"No worries. Get better!"

---

WHEN I LOOK at my phone again, there are three missed calls from Stephen. My lungs freeze with worry. *He never calls me repeatedly like this.*

I check the voice mail he left. "I'm so sorry, Raven," he says. "This meeting is going so far over. I need you to pick up Libby. Call me as soon as you can."

I look at my phone screen, noting the time. She's out of school *now*. There's no way I'm going to get to her in time. *Dammit, Stephen!* I make my excuses to Jana, not caring if she wants to fire me at this point.

All I care about is getting to Libby. I race through traffic, calling Stephen back as I drive. "I'm trying not to be mad at you," I say, leaving him a voice mail. "I'm on my way to get her now."

By the time I get to her school, most of the parking lot is empty. I race across to the front lawn, where Libby normally waits for me. When I see her, my breath catches with a mixture of relief and terror.

Mitch is with her and all I can think is how much it reminds me of *then*.

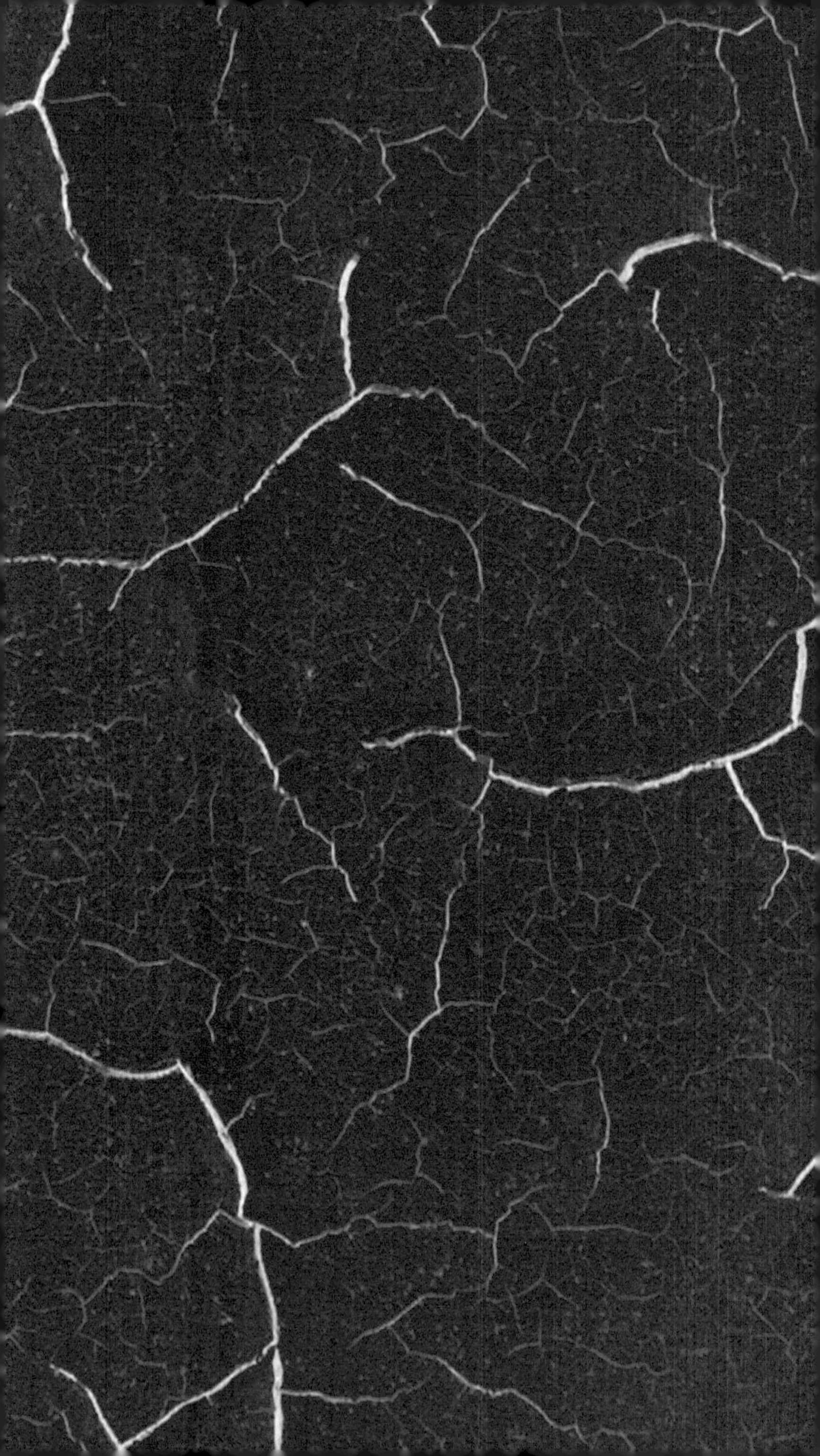

# 17

# RAVEN

### Then

I NEVER THOUGHT I'd miss riding the bus. It's so crowded and stuffy and *uncomfortable*, but lately, when I watch it pass through Mitch's passenger seat window, I imagine a time when I was able to ride without someone's hand between my thighs.

I haven't had to ride the bus in months. Mitch picks me up and drops me off—both to school and work. I don't know how he finds the time to do it, but it's really—thoughtful of him. He wants to make sure I'm safe and *comfortable.*

His fingers are resting against my jeans. Beneath the denim, I'm on fire. I try not to squirm, not to push him away. It will be so embarrassing for the both of us—I figured that out already.

"Your mom's okay with you closing tonight?" he asks.

I clear my throat. "Actually, she wanted me home earlier, if that's OK. I have finals in the morning."

When Mitch doesn't speak, I turn to look at him. His

lips are flattened into a thin line and his knuckles are white on the steering wheel. My breath starts to come in shallow bursts. "Actually, it doesn't matter. I already studied anyway."

He looks skeptical but some of the tension has already gone. "Are you sure?"

"Yeah." I give him a big, fake smile.

He grins in return. "I knew you wouldn't be able to say no."

My throat bobs. I swallow the bile that rises as his fingers move farther up.

<hr>

MITCH PARKS a few blocks from work to let me out. We wouldn't want anyone to know about *our little secret.* I'm alone again, almost to the front doors, when I notice my best friend is there waiting for me.

"Devin? What are you doing here?"

"I just—" He shrugs. "I wanted to see how you are."

"I'm... fine... you saw me at school today...."

"I know, but you've been acting different and I'm worried. I don't want to embarrass you. I know you won't talk to me with everyone else around and I just thought —" He sighs. "I don't know. I guess I hoped you would tell me now how you really feel and not that you're *fine.*" He frowns at me. "You've been so—distant. I just need to know you're okay."

I can feel my face turning red, not from him calling me out like this, but from thinking that if he knew the truth, he would want nothing to do with me anymore. "That's ridic—" I start to say, but Mitch's face appears in the window behind Devin.

My mouth falls open. I lose my train of thought, forgetting the denial that was just on my lips.

Devin's eyebrows shoot up. "What's wrong?" His head whips around to see what caught my attention.

"Nothing! I just—I remembered how late I am to clock in."

He looks skeptical. "Are you sure?"

"Yeah. I'm sorry, I'll talk to you about it later. Promise."

"Tonight?"

"No. I have to work late. Tomorrow." I smile to hide what I'm really saying inside. *Save me.*

"Fine," he says, moving to give me a hug.

Mitch is still watching us. I lean forward to give Devin an awkward pat on the back and pull away fast, before it can even be called a hug. He looks at me with a mixture of hurt and confusion but says nothing else before walking away.

Inside, I expect Mitch to say something but he's no longer there, he's moved on to do other things. I breathe a sigh of relief. A confrontation about Devin is not what I want. Mitch doesn't need to know anything about him.

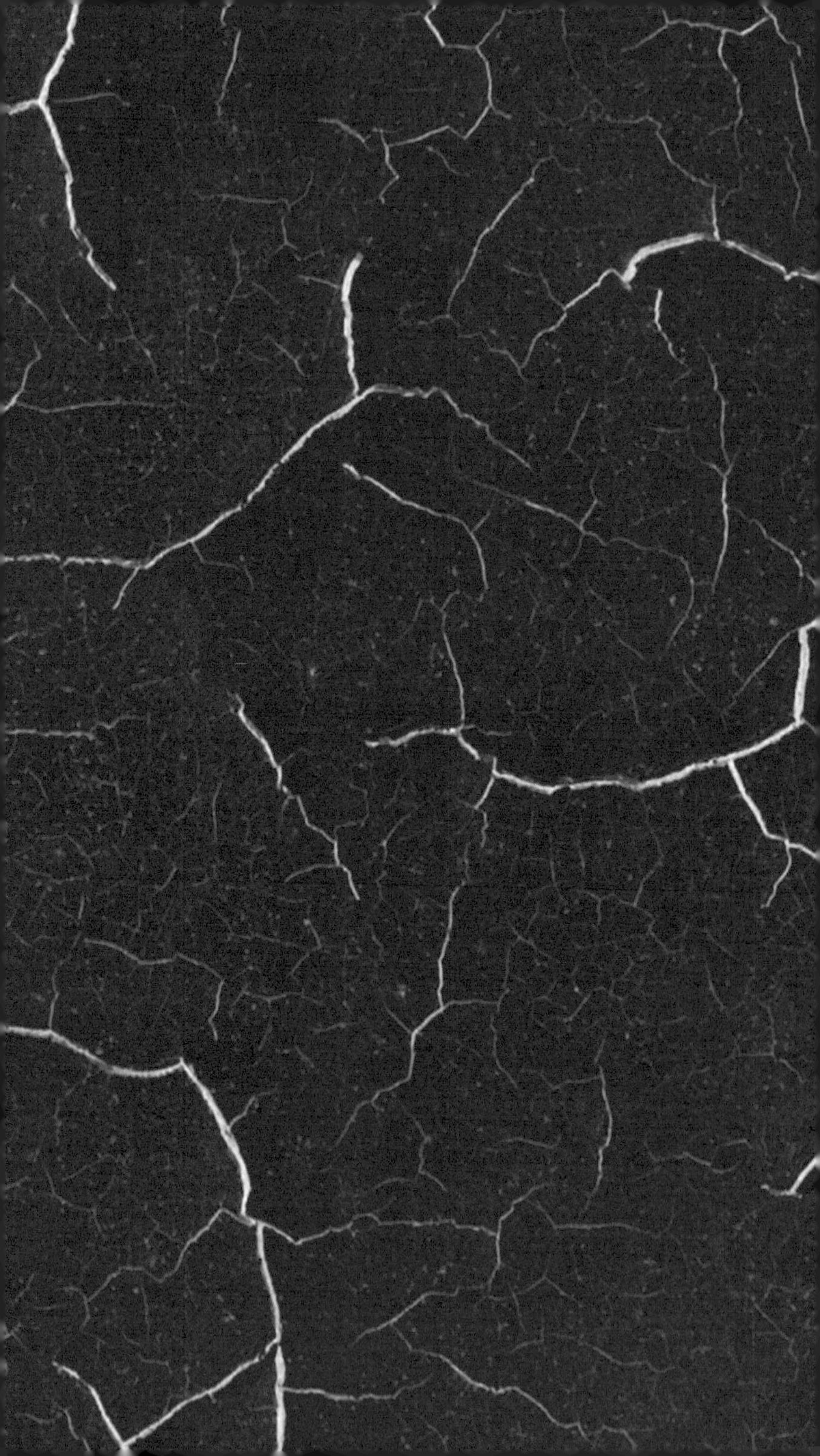

# 18

## NOW

### Mitch

I HAVEN'T SEEN her look this upset in years. I've almost forgotten how much I love to see that look on her face. The anger and fear mixed together into something absolutely breathtaking. Her eyes are lit up in a way that's so rare, her hair mussed, even her clothes look out of sorts.

"Mitch," she says slowly, trying to maintain her calm in front of Libby.

I grin at her. "You don't have to thank me. I just wanted to help in any way that I could. Libby was so worried when no one showed up for her."

"I don't want you to *ever* come near my daughter again." Raven's cheeks are pink now. She says the words through a clenched jaw.

I tilt my head. "I thought you didn't have any kids?"

Her lips thin. She doesn't respond.

"You must mean *my* daughter?" I push.

At the question, her eyes bulge and her pink cheeks change to a deep red. "She's not yours—"

"I beg to differ. Look at those blue eyes, Raven."

"No. You're wrong, Mitch. She's not yours!"

"Hmm," I say with a hand under my chin, pretending to think. "You know that *Stephen* is pretty loose-lipped when he's had too much to drink." I sober. "I know she's not his."

Raven's eyes dart to where Libby plays in the grass with another girl. She looks back to me on the verge of panic. "You're wrong."

"I can demand a paternity test."

"I don't know who the hell put that idea into your head, but you have no right—"

"I have every right! All these years, Raven! And you try to *hide* her from me—" I shake my head.

"It's not what you think. I'm telling you, you have this all wrong."

"The hell I do."

"You're not going to put us through this. I won't let you."

I take a step closer to her, rub a hand up her arm slowly.

She shivers at the touch, gooseflesh rises on her skin.

"Of course you will," I whisper.

Raven starts to shake her head in protest.

I bend to kiss her before she can say another word. Blood rushes through me as my heart pumps in overdrive. *I've been waiting for this for so long.*

Raven stills in my arms, doesn't protest.

I smile against her lips. *I knew she was waiting for me too.* I push myself against her so she can feel how much I want her. So she can know she still has that effect on me. *Nothing* has changed between us.

When I finally pull away, she fumbles, and I have to

catch her before she falls. Her eyes are wide, with so much going through that head of hers I can almost laugh. "Don't worry," I say. "It'll be our little secret. Just like before."

Only when a tear falls from her eye do I pause. *Why is she crying? She wants this as much as I do.* "Raven," I start, reaching for her.

She flinches, pulls from me. When I try again, she holds up her hands. "Don't—"

"I don't understand."

In a low voice, she says, "I do not want you, Mitch. I am happy with Stephen. Leave us *alone* or I'm going to call the police." She turns to leave without saying another word.

I watch her grab Libby by the arm and lead her to the car. My teeth grind together the entire time. I could go to her, stop her, try again. *Now's my chance.*

I clench my fists. No. It's *Stephen.* He's in the way —*blinding* her. Just like all the others did before.

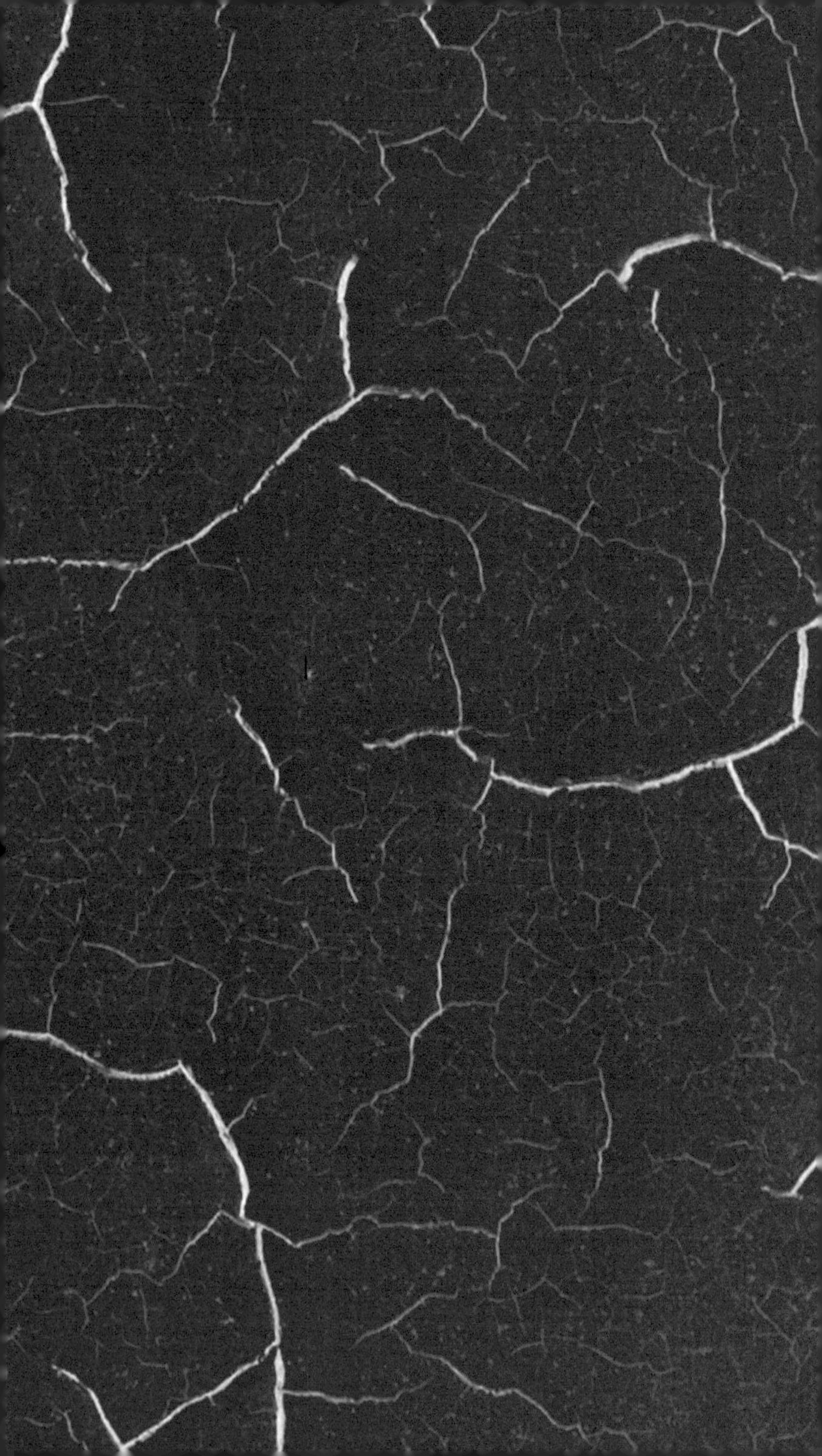

19

---

## MITCH

Then

SHE'S BEEN SEEING this *kid*. After seeing them together, I had to make sure, and once again, I'm glad I trusted my instincts. Raven holds this *loser's* hand, cries into his shoulder. He wraps his scrawny arms around her, and I clench my fists so hard my knuckles crack. The sight of them makes me sick.

First Kyle, then Aaron, now this *boy*. It seems Raven is a little hussy. How many more will she draw to her like moths to the flame? I know I'm just another of her moths, and yet, I can't stay away.

*What would her little boyfriend think about her if he knew what she was doing with me after work almost every night?* I grin at the thought. Raven is *mine*, and it's time they both learn it.

RAVEN IS LOOKING out the window, per her usual. She likes to people-watch as I drive. My hand rests between her thighs, per my usual.

I wiggle my fingers a little to get her attention. She gasps and looks at me. I can't help but smile at her reaction. "Do you know that kid?" I ask, pointing at a bony boy riding his bike alone, his handlebars full of books. *The kid I know she more than knows.*

He's far ahead of us, but if I know him from this distance, I know she does too. He's alone, on a side street and there are no other cars around. *No witnesses.*

Raven's face drains of color. Her eyes widen, but she's trying to hide the shock. She gives a little headshake. "No. He probably goes to my school."

My smile widens. *What a little liar!*

"Why?" she asks. "Did he apply for a job?"

"It looks like he's in trouble."

She turns to look at me, no longer bothering to hide her emotions. Her hand flies to mine and I dig my fingers harder against her center.

"Please, Mitch," she whispers.

We're nearing the boy. I'm going nice and slow, but Raven starts to sense the danger. The boy seems to, too, pedaling harder. She grasps me like her life depends on it.

"Please, what?" I ask, my eyebrow raised.

She rocks her hips against my hand. *Trying to distract me.* "Sorry, love. That won't work this time."

"Mitch, no!" Raven screams as I floor the gas, turn the steering wheel, and plow into the boy. There's a sickening thud and crunch as we roll over his body, but I keep the accelerator pressed, and we continue on our way.

"Did you hear that? Must've been a cat in the road."

She turns to look behind us, sobbing freely.

"Damn thing should've kept in his lane."

Raven won't look at me, but that's okay. I'll let her be upset for now. She has to understand, I'm only looking out for her best interests. These moths... they'll overwhelm her if they're not taken care of.

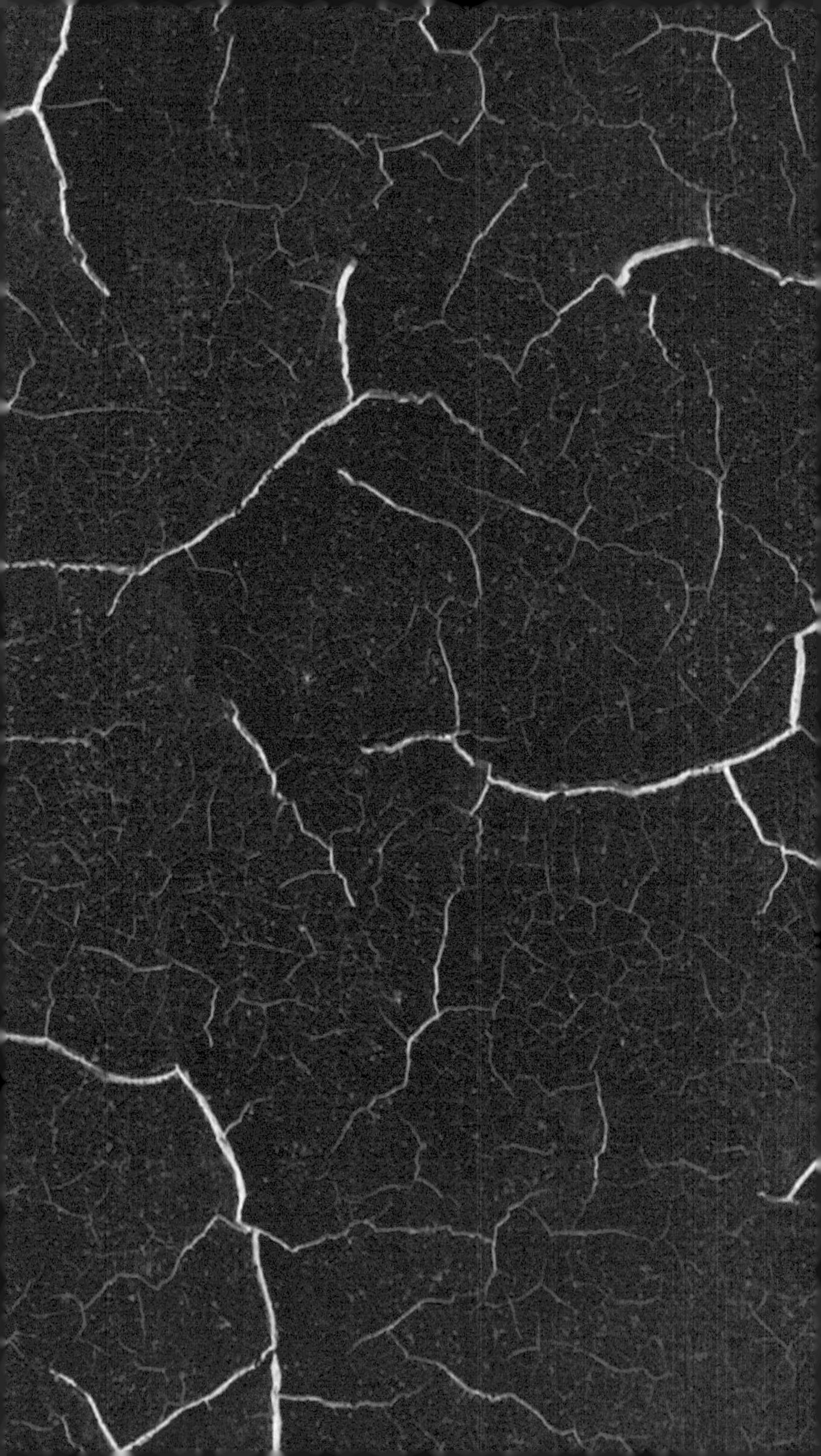

20

———

MITCH

Now

THIS TIME, I'm not going to be so damned rash. I'm going to cover my bases, make sure there are no witnesses and make sure I'm not caught like an idiot, *like before*. And I have a little tool up my sleeve to help me do just that.

———

"ANOTHER ROUND!" Jack calls to the bartender, raising his empty glass. He doesn't seem to notice that she's not listening and couldn't even hear his drunken request over the noise from this far away.

I smile indulgently at him. "I'll go grab it."

"Hey, what a guy!" Jack cries. "Thanks, man, I owe you one."

"My pleasure," I say. I raise an eyebrow at the rest of our group. "Anyone else up for another?"

Stephen shakes his head. "None for me, thanks."

"Party pooper!" Jack's date cries at him. She reaches to give him a playful smack on the shoulder but misses, only hitting air. "You're too far away!" she complains, laughing.

Jack laughs like it's the funniest thing he's heard all day. "You—'re," he hiccups. "You're hilarious."

She beams at him before drunkenly leaning against him, letting her hands move up his chest.

Stephen, who's less than an arm's length from her, only smiles at their ridiculousness.

"I'll just be right back, then," I say, grinning on my way to the bar.

"I really should be going," Stephen says, stopping me.

"Aww! Just one more!" she cries.

"Yeah, one more!" Jack agrees.

They start chanting together, "One more, one more, one more...."

Stephen ducks his head in embarrassment. "Okay, okay, stop. I'll stay for one more, then I have to go."

I head for the bar. *This one's on me, Stephen, buddy.*

WE WALK OUT AS A GROUP, Jack and his date both three sheets to the wind. "I'll drive," Stephen says. "I only had the two."

"Non—sense," Jack says. "I dri—ve ca—an." He breaks into laughter. "I mean—I can drive."

"I think Stephen is right here," I chime in. "I'll take your date home. I don't mind."

She giggles at me. "That's so thoughtful."

Jack pouts. "I was hoping to..." He wiggles his eyebrows. "You know..."

She giggles again, then doubles over and vomits on Jack's shoes. She looks up at him with tears in her eyes. "I'm so sorry." She stumbles a few feet and heaves again.

"Right," Stephen says. "So, I'll drive Jack home and you take her?"

I nod. "No problem."

We get into our respective vehicles and head our own ways. *Or so Stephen thinks.*

We're at an intersection—on a cliff—Jack's date already long passed out in back, when I T-bone his car at full force. They roll down the side of the hill, slamming into tree after tree, until finally stopping in the valley below.

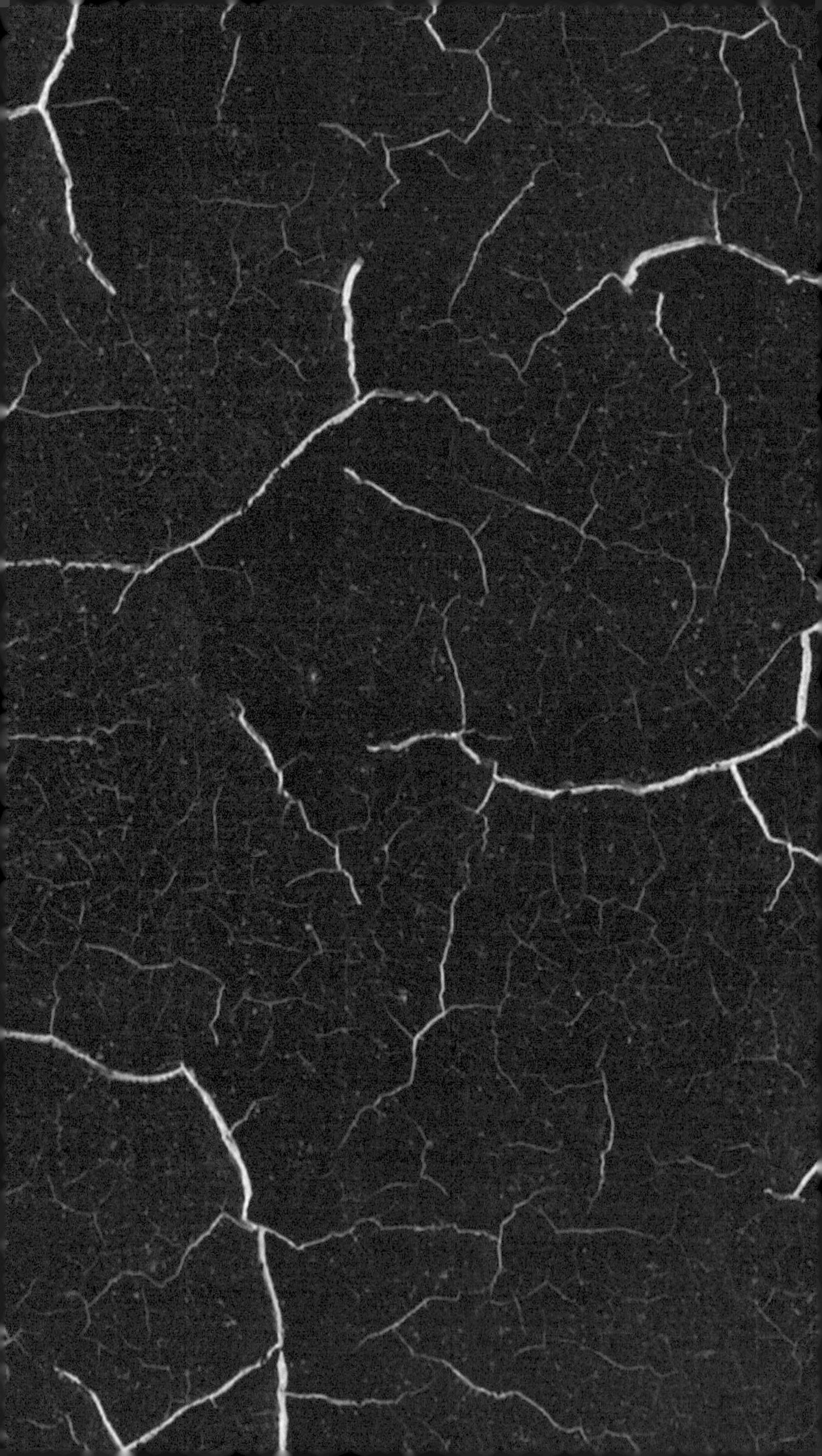

# MITCH

Then

THINGS HAVE BEEN SO MUCH BETTER with Raven; I almost want to kick myself for not acting sooner. Her reaction has been better than I could've imagined. Now that she's out of school, she stays to close every shift, instead of only occasionally.

We don't have to spend all our time sneaking around in my truck, either. She's able to come home with me. And perhaps even better, she stays far away from other *males*. Even with customers, she keeps her distance. No more inappropriate touching.

I'm watching her now, through the kitchen doors. She's avoiding a table full of high schoolers, all eyeing her as she keeps walking past them. She hasn't stopped to help them once, even with them all needing refills.

Crystal stops her. I read her lips asking, "Can you help me out with table seven?"

Raven shakes her head. "I'm sorry, I can't."

Crystal frowns at her. "Why not?"

"Sorry," Raven says again, walking away without any explanation.

A smile forms on my lips. *Good girl.* Of course I need my customers to be happy, and get the best service, but more importantly, Raven is learning how to behave. Satisfied, I move to check on my kitchen staff.

"Mitch?" A hand brushes against my back in a slow caress. I jump in surprise at the contact before frowning down at Nessa.

"Can I help you?" I ask, giving her an annoyed look.

"There's someone up front who wants to speak with you."

I can't help but sigh. *Another impatient customer, who thinks complaining to the boss is going to get them a table sooner.* "Alright. Who is it?" I ask, motioning for her to lead the way.

It's crowded up front. Business is good. I look from face to face, expecting an angry patron to step forward. I look to Nessa with eyebrows raised.

She shrugs. "He must be outside. I'll just check."

A moment later, my breath catches as two men step inside behind Nessa. I can tell from the way they're dressed, and the expressions on their faces, that they're no ordinary customers.

"Are you Mitchell Murphy?" one asks.

"I am. Can I help you?" I glance around us, noticing everyone in the waiting area has gone quiet, staring now.

"I'm Detective Rossi, and this is my partner, Detective Gill." He flashes a badge. "We have a couple of questions for you, if you wouldn't mind stepping outside with us for a few minutes."

My jaw clenches automatically. I try to relax but I find myself incapable. "I'm sorry, detectives, I really don't have the time today. As you can see, we're slammed. If you could come back another day, I'd love to speak with you about..." I raise an eyebrow. "Whatever it is you're interested in."

The men look at each other and then the one who hasn't spoken yet, Gill, takes a step toward me. He leans forward, saying softly, "You're under arrest, Murphy. We can either do this the embarrassing way or the slightly less embarrassing way. It's up to you."

I flinch at the words but give a tense nod. I look back to Nessa, who's staring with wide eyes. "I'm going to step outside with these gentlemen, it'll be a few minutes."

"O-OK, Mitch." She nods.

"Right then, shall we?" I say to Detective Gill.

"After you," he says, opening the door for me.

They arrest me there on the sidewalk, a few steps from the doors. I look through the back seat window to see Raven's face absent of all color, watching as they take me away.

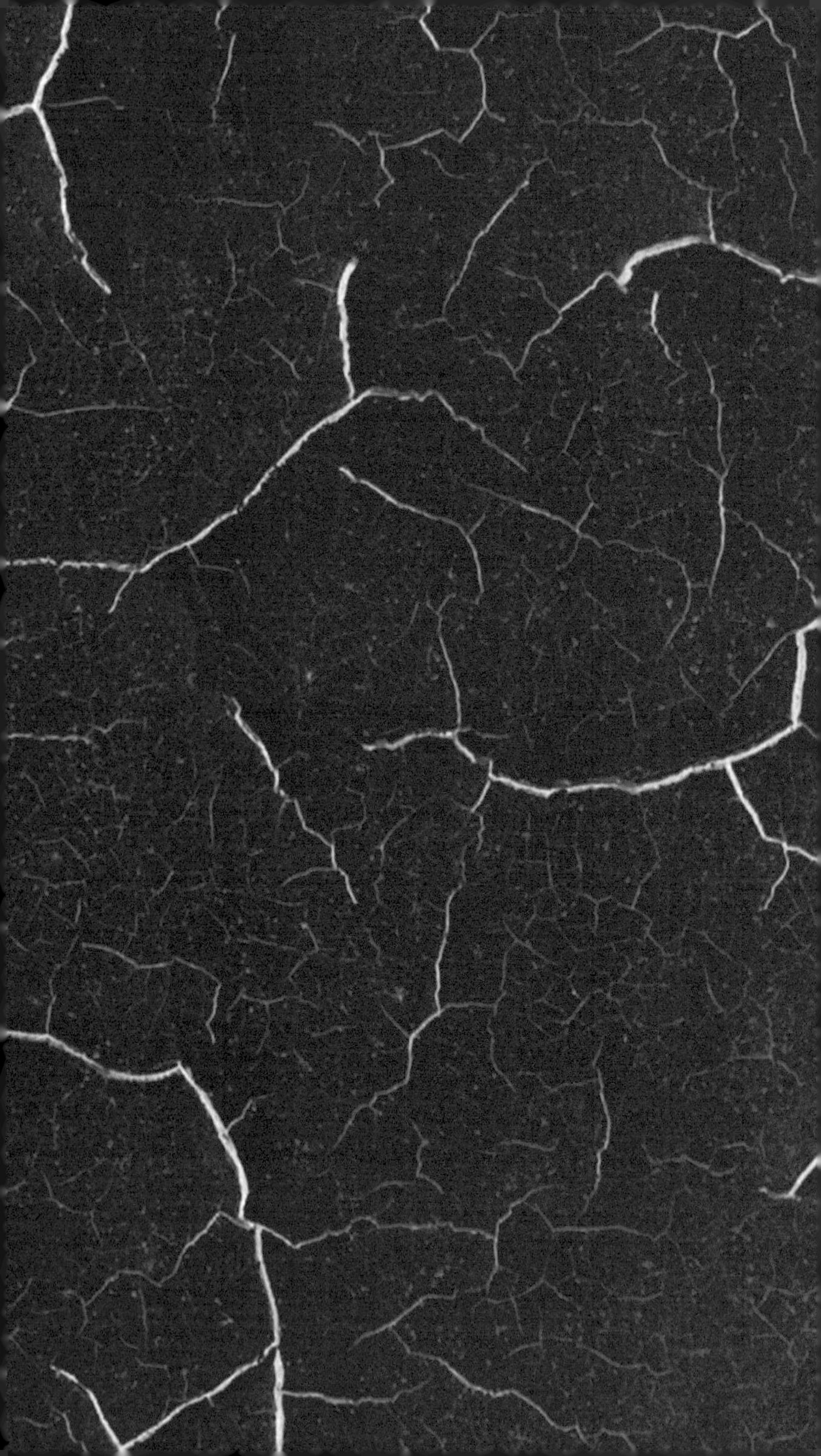

# 22

## RAVEN

Now

I BRUSH Stephen's hair back from his face. My tears fall on his cold cheek, and I brush them away too. The heart rate monitor beeps, filling the silence.

Stephen starts to stir. I wipe my face before he opens his eyes.

"Raven?"

"It's me, I'm here." I grip his hand in mine. "I'm so, so sorry." More tears push forward, breaking past the carefully constructed dam.

He reaches a weak hand up to my face. "It's not your fault. It never was."

"This is the second time," I say between sobs. "You're not a cat. You don't have nine lives."

He chuckles and then winces at the pain it causes. "Don't make me laugh," he groans.

"I should've known he would do this. Why didn't you tell me he found you?" I demand. I'm trying not to be angry with him, but I can't help feeling a little betrayed he hid this from me.

"He didn't know me. I thought—God, I don't know what I thought." Stephen clenches his eyes shut. "I thought I could outsmart him, stop him, figure him out. I don't know, Raven." He looks at me with shining eyes. "I'm sorry."

I pull down the covers from his chest to examine the scars—old and new. "He's trying to tear you to pieces," I whisper.

"He's an idiot. Can't even kill a guy properly."

I glare at him with a slack jaw. *He hasn't heard about Jack.*

He grows sober at my expression.

My fingers tighten around his hand. "I'm so sorry, Stephen."

Stephen shakes his head. "No, no. Please tell me—not Jack."

I give a slight nod.

He clenches his eyes shut while crying out. "God, it's all my fault!"

"It's not. Don't do that to yourself."

"I knew I was playing with fire. Didn't even warn him!"

I sit on the edge of his bed while we sob into each other's shoulders. "Why didn't I just tell him to go to hell the minute I saw him?" I ask. "I invited him in, played along with his little game—"

Stephen runs a hand through my hair. "Because you knew he would find you anyway. And you knew he would do this. Even as bad as it is, it could've been worse."

I bite my lip to stifle the crying. I try to believe he's

right, *It could've been worse.* Even if that's true, we both know Mitch isn't done yet.

"We should've changed my name too. Why didn't we do that? I feel like such a fool."

"Welcome to the club, babe. Look on the bright side. At least we have all his money. *That's* kinda nice, isn't it?"

I can't help but grimace. On one hand, yeah, it is kinda nice. And I love my car, so there's that... but on the other hand, I hate knowing that *his* money is supporting us. *His* money is giving us the lifestyle we live. It's almost like he's still *taking care of me.* What would Mitch do if he found out who Stephen really is?

"It's your money," I remind him *and myself.*

"Yeah," Stephen says. He goes to stretch, then winces.

"I'll get the doctor," I say.

"Wait." Stephen looks up at me, more solemn than I've ever seen. "First, we need to talk about what we're going to do."

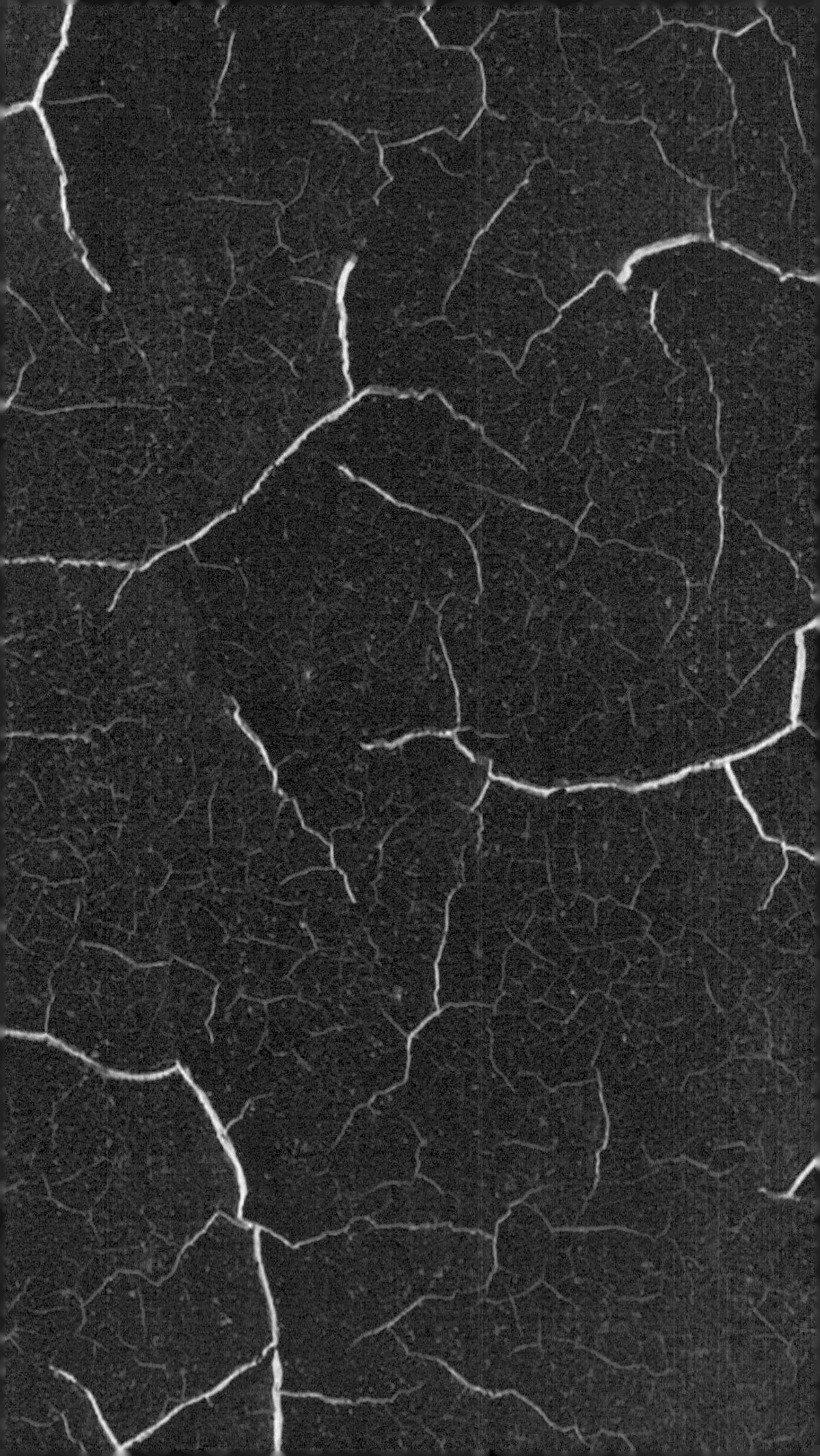

## 23

## MITCH

Then

"I'm not angry with you," I say, *lying*. "I understand you were only frightened. It's my fault; I don't blame you."

It's quiet on the other end of the line for a few seconds before Raven says, "Mitch, it wasn't me."

My hand clenches the receiver so hard the plastic grinds. "It's okay. You don't have to lie about it."

"I'm not—"

"And just so you know, the kid isn't dead."

Silence again and then, "He—he's not?"

"Nope. If he was, they would've arrested me for murder instead of attempted murder."

The only sound Raven makes is that of her crying.

"Anyway," I say, "I wanted to say thank you for taking my call. You didn't have to, and I can't tell you how glad I am to hear your voice." I imagine her holding the cell phone I bought her, wiping the tears from her cheeks. "Will you be at the trial?"

"Yes," she whispers.

It was a stupid question. *Of course she will be.* The question is: is she going to keep her mouth shut, or throw me under the bus? I clench my jaw, already knowing where this is headed.

"Listen. I need you to just listen to me for a minute, okay?" I wait for her to stop sniffling.

"Okay," she finally says.

"No matter what happens after the trial, whatever they sentence me to, I'll come for you after. I'll find you and we can pick up right where we left off."

Raven starts crying again.

I continue, "Don't ever blame yourself, okay? None of this is your fault."

"I know," she says.

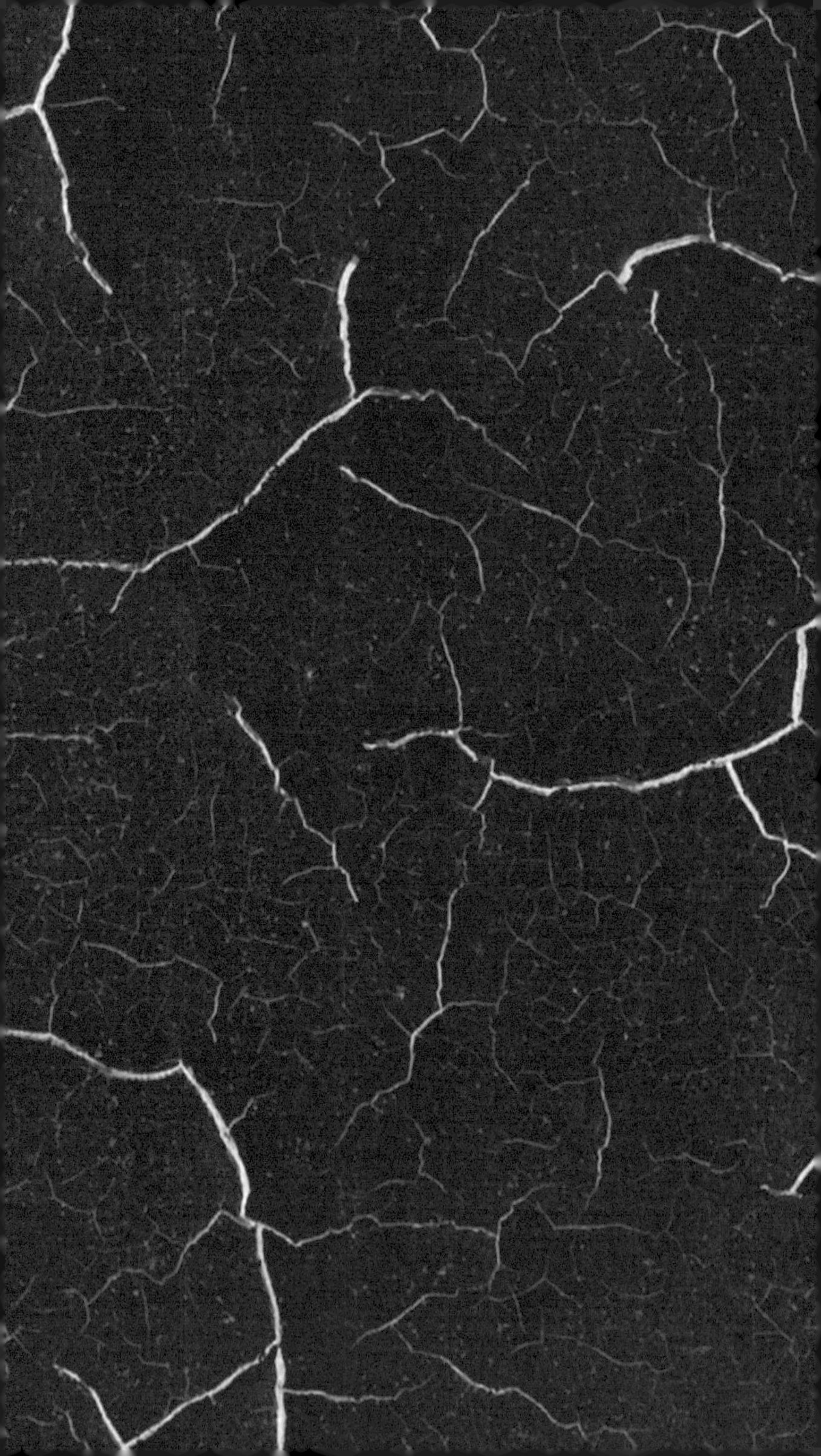

# RAVEN

Now

THE DOORBELL RINGS, making me jump. Whoever's there is insistent, pushing the button over and over. I'm terrified to answer the door. *It could be Mitch.* He tried to kill Stephen—there's no doubt in my mind he's coming for me next.

Lucky for me, I don't even have to go to the eyehole to see who's outside. Staying hidden in the bedroom, I pull up my doorbell application on my phone.

My friend Crystal, from work, stands on my front step holding a bouquet of flowers and what looks like a casserole. My cheeks flame at the sight. I haven't been to work since Stephen's accident and they're probably short staffed without me.

I press the button to speak. "Hang on, I'll be right out." I open the door for her, expecting to see a friendly smile or a look of concern on her face. Instead, I'm shocked to see she looks *angry*—pissed even.

"Crystal? Are you okay?"

She barks a laugh. "Oh, I'm *fine*. I take it your man isn't so hot, though."

Heat rises up my neck at her crude behavior. It's so out of the ordinary for her. She's never been like this, not even when I first met her years ago.

Crystal pushes past me without giving me a chance to invite her in. She looks around for a second, then spotting the kitchen, heads in that direction. "Nice place," she says.

I rush to close the door and follow her but before the latch clicks in place, the door pushes back at me. I'm caught off guard, too concerned with Crystal, too unfocused to notice she wasn't alone. The door swings at me and I barely have time to block my face from getting hit.

Mitch steps into my foyer. "Nice place, indeed, Raven."

My eyes go wide at the sight of him. My head swivels back to Crystal.

She gives me a grim smile, tilts her head. "Just figuring it out, sweetie?"

"Get out," I say. "Both of you. Now, before I call the police."

Neither of them move. Mitch looks at Crystal in a silent form of communication. She nods.

"I don't know what either of you wants. But I mean it. Get the hell out of my house." I reach for my phone but it's not in my pocket and I break out in a nervous sweat as I realize I don't have it.

"Missing something?" Crystal asks.

"Enough," Mitch says, giving Crystal a look. "Raven, you know I'm not here to hurt you."

I shake my head. "No. I don't know that at all."

He gives me a hurt look. "Our mutual friend"—he points to Crystal—"was the only way I knew I could find you and talk to you. I knew if I came alone that you would be too frightened."

That same word from five years ago slams into me. *Frightened.* I try to unlock my jaw so I can speak but it doesn't want to budge.

"Crystal is going to leave us now." He smiles. "She understands we need some privacy—some time to get... reacquainted. Properly." Mitch turns to Crystal. "Isn't that right?"

I notice she's no longer full of smug satisfaction. The anger I saw in her at the door is back in full force. She looks like she could easily murder me if he wasn't there to stop her.

"You can't just leave me with him!" I cry, finally finding my voice again. "Crystal, please."

Her eyes flash to mine. "Don't for one minute think that I'd pick you over him," she hisses. "Save your breath."

I flinch at her venom. I had no clue she felt this way, was—*in love* with him. Nessa's words from all that time ago come back. *He and Crystal have a thing, I guess.*

"Do you really think I just happened to *coincidentally* find a job at the same diner as you? Did you think in a city full of millions of people and thousands of restaurants, I was *so* limited in options that there was no place else to work, except with little ole you?" She grimaces at me. "God, you're so full of yourself. You're even worse now than back then."

"That's enough, I said," Mitch says. "Crystal, if you would, please." He motions for her to approach the front door.

She approaches, looking like she's going to be sick.

"Crystal," I beg again.

"Don't," she hisses.

Mitch pats her on the shoulder as she walks back outside. We're all alone and all I can think is, *thank God Libby isn't home to see this.*

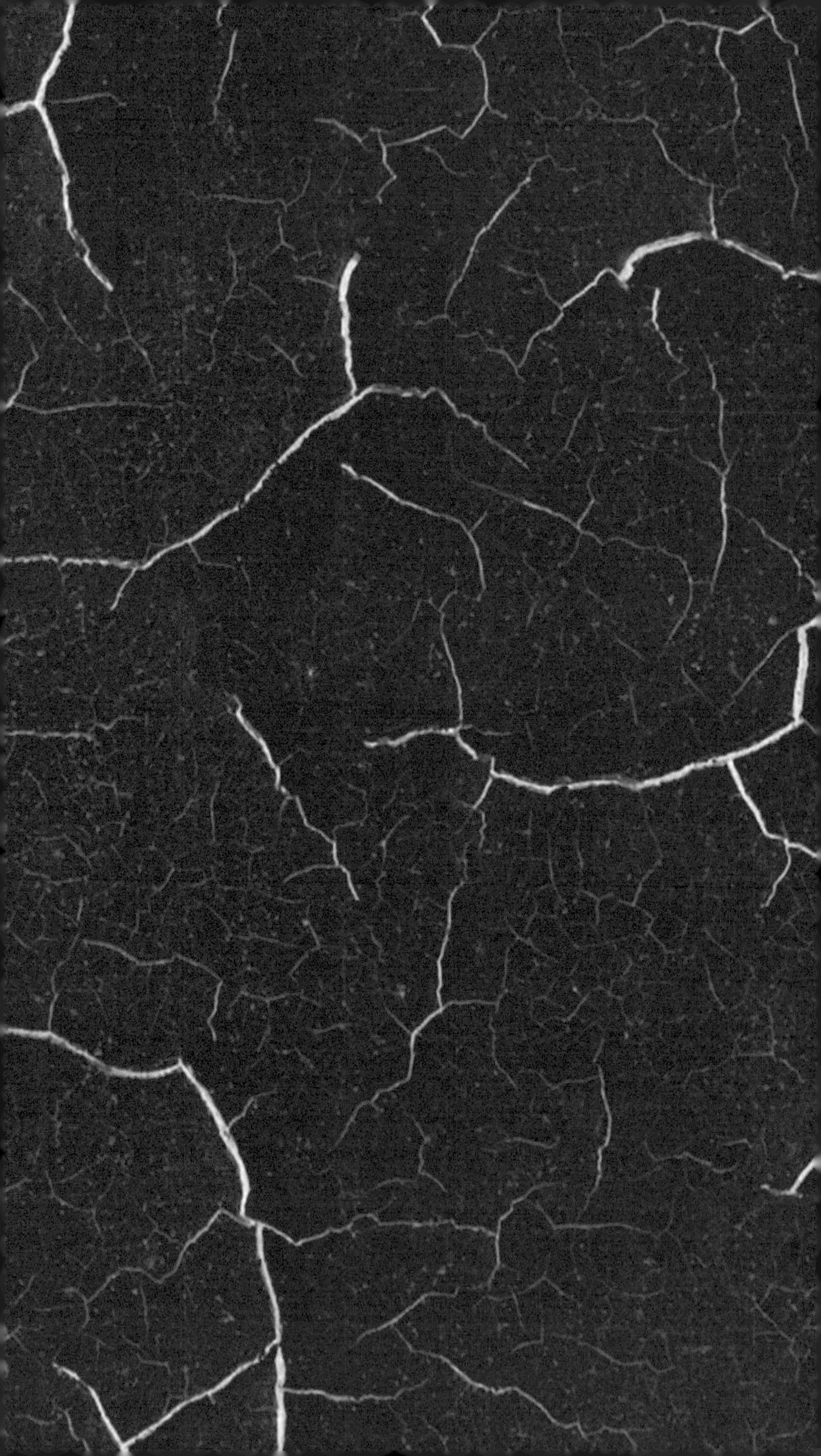

## MITCH

Then

IT'S HARD NOT to look behind me. I can feel her sitting there, silently waiting with me. Even though I can't see her, it's like I can reach back and touch her. *I want to. More than anything.*

I don't know which seat she's in, but I can hear her breathing. I can hear her gasp for breath in between tears, wipe them from her face when they fall. I close my eyes for a brief moment, giving in to the urge to picture her face.

Sweat trickles down my back as I wait. I took the plea deal. It was better than the alternative, or so I'm told.

"There's too much evidence," my attorney warned. "They'll flay you alive if you try to fight it."

I thought about protesting. I thought, *maybe Raven will keep her mouth shut after all.* But then I thought *she might not have a choice.*

"The court can subpoena anyone," my attorney informed me with a look. "Best not to put ideas into their heads. They might start asking questions we really don't want them to ask."

I got the picture. Things could get worse. Much worse. Neither my attorney nor I wanted an investigation into my relationship with Raven or any of the boys who conveniently left the picture. So, I took the deal.

The bailiff calls for us to rise as the judge enters. As I do, I can't help risking a glance behind me. Seconds tick by, adrenaline making me dizzy as I try to find her. I can't get caught looking at her, but I can't survive the next however many years without one last glimpse, either.

*Where is she? Where is she? There!*

I spot her, finally. Our eyes meet. Hers are red and swollen. Mine flick to see who's next to her. Some of the others from work are here—Nessa, Crystal, Dale.

My breath catches. To Raven's other side is the boy. *The one who's supposed to be dead.* He wraps an arm around her. She leans into his shoulder, never taking her eyes from mine.

An elbow to my side makes me turn back around. I clench my fists at my side, trying to keep calm. I can feel the anger—no, the *rage,* rising to my face. *Everything depends on playing my cards right.*

The judge breaks off into a lecture about how wrong I was, how irresponsible, how *stupid,* but then she goes on to express how she doesn't believe I'm evil and although I deserve to be punished, don't deserve to have the entire rest of my life taken away.

"As it's your first offense, and you've expressed your regret, which I believe to be sincere, the court sentences you to incarceration no less than sixty months for assault in the first degree." She lists a bunch of legal jargon that goes over my head, then hammers her gavel to seal the deal.

The boy's parents are outraged at my "slap on the wrist," some people yell, some whisper among themselves. I try to look, to find her in the mass but I can't. I'm led away before I have the chance to see her again.

"Mitch!" a voice calls.

I fight against the guards to look.

Crystal stands out, staring at me. "I'll be here," she says.

There's nothing to say. I give in to the guards as they lead me through the doors.

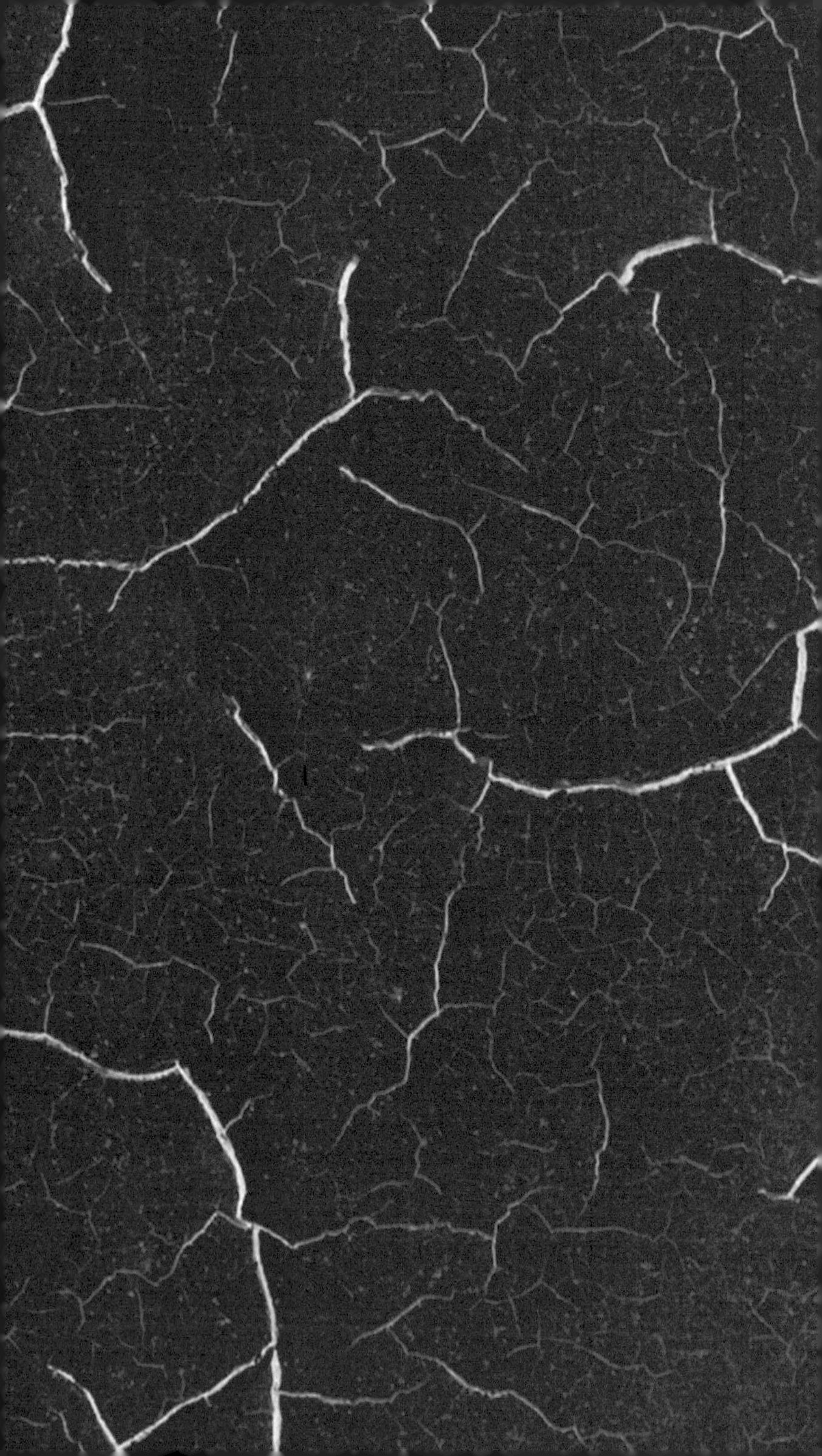

## MITCH

Now

THIS IS IT—THE moment I've been waiting for, for over five years. I'm so excited, I'm nearly shaking. It's just us now, and I can do *anything* I want to her.

Part of me wants to throttle her. *How good that would feel to take my anger out on her.* But I know that's wrong. I could never do that. Besides, it's not her I want to throttle. It's *him.*

Raven takes a step away from me and then another. I let her distance herself. *For now.*

"Where's Libby?" I ask.

She flinches, thinks about how to answer. "I need to pick her up from school soon."

I smile. "You know, you have a bad habit of lying, Raven."

She flushes.

"You still think you can keep her from me, don't you?"

"She's not yours!"

"Just like you're not, right?"

Raven glares at me, so red she looks like an overripe tomato. She's so adorable when she's this pissed. All I want to do is kiss her.

"Please leave," she says.

"I'm not going anywhere, Raven. I've waited too long for this." I take a step toward her. She looks like a frightened little lamb, ready to bolt.

I take another slow step and she backs away at the same pace I go forward. She's backing herself into the kitchen, *into a wall.* I let her, enjoying the game of cat and mouse.

"I never understood why," I say. "I mean, I know you were frightened after that incident with the truck, but did you even realize what you were doing to me? Did you understand that you were ruining my life?" I throw my hands up. "Things could've been so different. Libby could've had her father in her life!"

"She does already!" Raven reaches for the knife block on the counter. "Get away from me!" she yells.

I rush toward her, trying to stop her before she can grab one but she's too fast. She rips one of the knives out, slicing my arm as I reach for her. Raven gapes as my blood pours out onto her kitchen floor.

While she's distracted, I move, backhanding her so hard she stumbles. As she tries to keep herself from falling, I knock the knife from her hand and wrap my own uninjured one around her throat. All I can think of is how beautiful she looks with those wild eyes that would rip me apart if they could.

She's pinned in place, doesn't even try to move, knows it's pointless. I bend to kiss her, and she opens for me, sighing into my mouth as I take my claim. *Finally.*

The pain comes sudden and full force. I pull back

from her, crying out as a knife is plunged into my back and then ripped back out of me with the same unforgiving force.

"Run, Raven!" a man yells. *Stephen.*

He's here, pulling her away from me. *No, no, no!* "Aren't you supposed to be dead?" I growl.

"Don't come near us," he says, holding the bloody knife in one hand, a gun in the other.

There's no choice. He's going to take her from me, and I won't have another chance. It's now or never.

I lunge at him with everything that I have. This *man* is still practically a *boy*. And he hasn't been in prison. He doesn't stand a chance.

The gun goes off, shooting a hole in the ceiling. The recoil takes him off guard and he loses his grip. It's not hard to knock it from him. After that, it's only a matter of getting the knife.

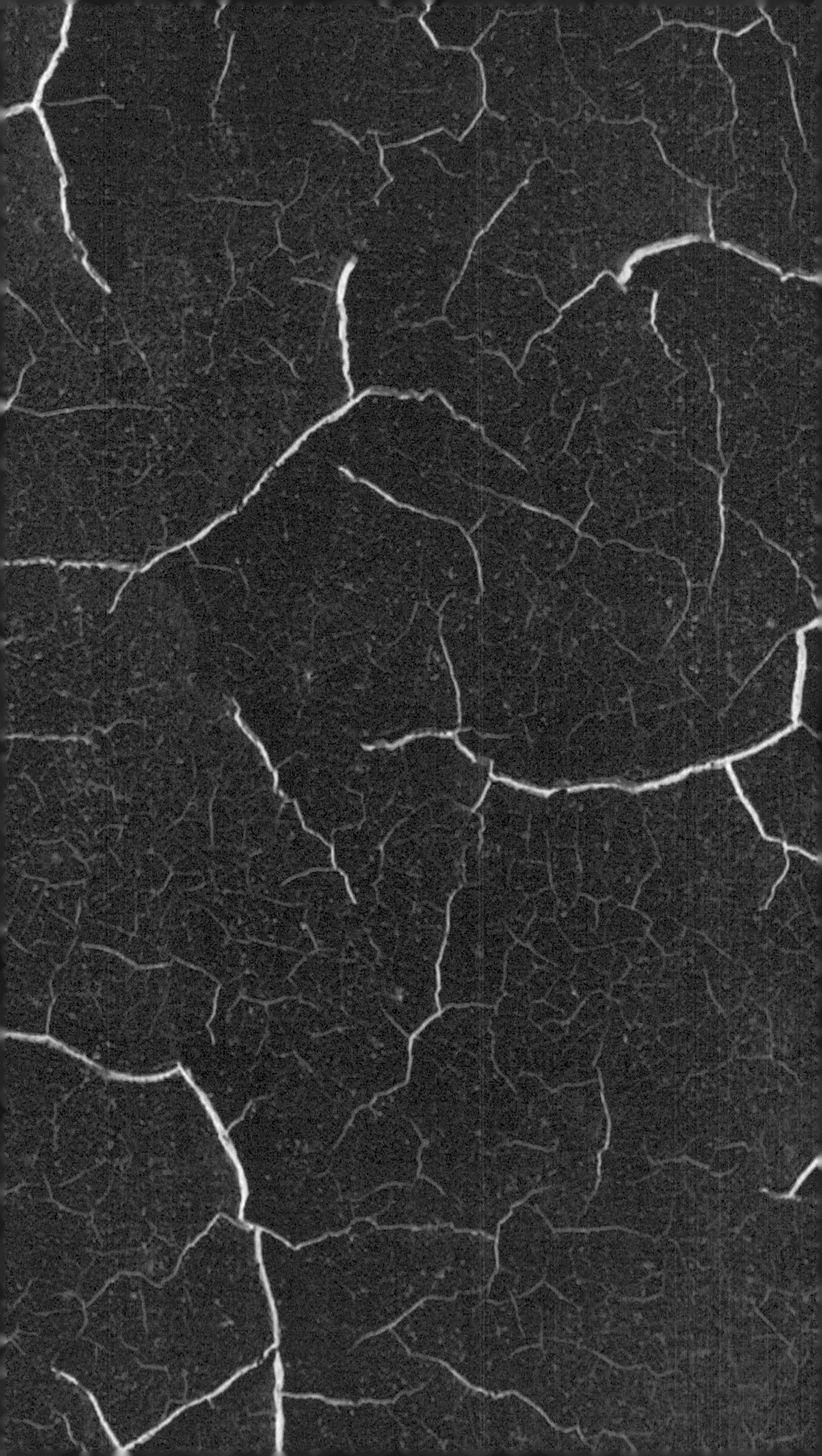

# RAVEN

Now

MITCH ATTACKS STEPHEN at full force. They fall to the floor, fists flying at each other's faces.

"Stephen, no!" I cry. Some of his stitches have been ripped open and are bleeding.

Mitch notices too. He reaches to dig into one of Stephen's open wounds. Blood spreads through the fabric of his shirt. When he reels back in pain, it's all Mitch needs to get the upper hand.

The gun is on the floor and within seconds, the knife joins it. I look around for something—*anything* that might help. They're practically rolling around on top of the weapons. There's no way I can grab either of them.

I have to do something to stop this, something to distract Mitch, give Stephen a chance to get out from under him. "Libby is your daughter!" I scream.

At first he doesn't seem to hear me. He shows no reaction, only keeps struggling with Stephen

I continue, "Don't go to jail again. Don't leave us again, Mitch."

He stops, looks up at me. He's—crying.

I'm so taken aback, I almost don't know what to say. Of all the reactions, I didn't expect this. I almost feel bad for lying to him. *Almost.*

Just when I think he's done fighting, he reaches into his pocket and pulls out zip ties. Stephen doesn't have a chance to get away before Mitch has his wrists bound behind his back.

"Mitch, don't!" I cry.

"Don't worry, Raven. We're going to give him a good show. Right before I kill him."

"Like hell we are!" I run for the door, willing to call out for help to the whole neighborhood if I have to.

Mitch grabs a fistful of my hair and yanks my head back. "You're not going anywhere, love," he whispers, slipping a zip tie around my wrists too.

Tears pool in my eyes. "Mitch, please don't do this. You don't have to do this."

He cups my chin in his hand, brushes away a stray tear with his thumb. "Hey, it's okay. You don't have to say anything." He leads me into the living room, and as he lays me down on the couch, he says, "Did you really think I didn't know who he was?"

"Wh—what are you—"

Mitch barks a laugh. "Enough lying! You know damn well what I'm talking about. *Stephen* is your little boyfriend. The one we ran over in the truck. The one who *sued me* for everything I'm worth. The one *giving you a life! My fucking life!*"

"Don't you touch her!" Stephen screams from the kitchen.

I grimace at the fury on Mitch's face.

He slips off his shoes, holds up one of his socks, and says, "Hold that thought." He goes to Stephen, hits him over and over before shoving the sock in his mouth.

"As I was saying," he huffs. "I'm actually glad he's not dead from the crash. He needs to suffer a little before he dies. And—" He strokes my hair. "He can see how much pleasure I can give you."

Bile rises in my throat. I try to scoot back, distance myself from him, but he holds me in place. Mitch kneels.

Stephen screams through his gag.

I feel light-headed and nauseous.

A pounding comes at the door.

All of us turn to look. The pounding comes again. "This is the police! Open up!"

Mitch turns to meet my gaze. "It wasn't you, after all, was it?"

I shake my head. "I tried to tell you."

The door breaks in. Police officers come in, pointing their guns at Mitch, yelling, "Hands up!" and "Get down!"

My world is spinning. I dry heave as they take him away.

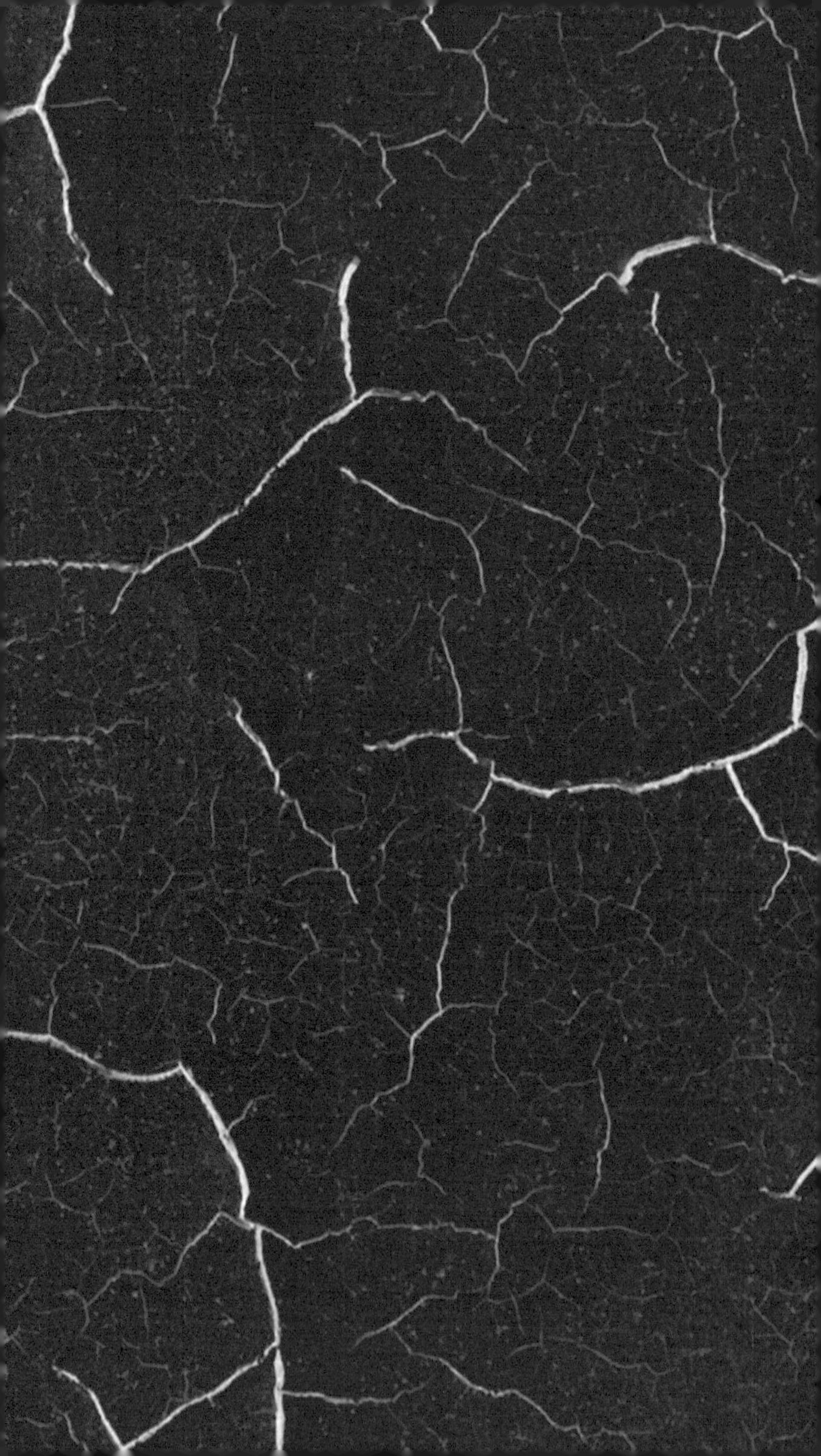

## RAVEN

Now

CRYSTAL IS WAITING FOR ME. I think about telling the police, "She's the one you want, too!" but did she even do anything wrong? *If it wasn't for her calling the police*—I shudder at the thought.

When the police and the ambulance and everyone else are gone, I go to her.

"He was doing it again," she says. "It was me and then it was you. I felt thrown away, used, garbage, *old*."

"Crystal, I never knew."

She shakes her head. "He didn't want you to know."

"I wasn't—" I gulp. "I—"

"You don't have to say anything. I already know." She stares into my eyes, saying nothing when the tears come. She lets me cry and she's possibly the only person alive who understands.

"When I saw him hit that boy with his truck, I knew I had to do something."

I gasp. "You saw?"

She nods.

"You didn't say anything—"

"I did though." She gives me a knowing look. And it dawns on me. She's the one who turned him in.

"I saw him this time too. I was in the back, supposed to be passed out."

I reach for her hand. "You're stronger than I am, Crystal."

Crystal shakes her head. "No. I'm not." She wipes a tear from her cheek. "I've been so eager to please him, so anxious to get one more look, one more touch, the way it used to be. I've been willing to do anything he asked of me. Even back then, I got Nessa to bring you to that party. I would've fucked your man's friend too, if Mitch wanted me to."

She runs her hands through her hair, growling at herself. "I've been his plaything—his *accomplice*. I knew what he was doing, and it didn't matter. The only thing that mattered was the satisfied look he gave me when I did something right."

I clench my teeth together, willing my heart rate to slow down. What she's telling me—without her help, maybe it would've been different. All those times I turned to her, wanting to quit or to call out—the words of encouragement she gave me.

"I was you not very long ago," she says. "And then you had your daughter—"

"She's not his."

"I know." She smiles. "Mitch is an idiot for not seeing how much she looks like Stephen."

I don't know what to say, so I say nothing.

"I think—maybe he never really wanted me to just do his bidding—he wanted me to have a backbone," she continues. "Well, here I am, finally able to stand up on my own, think for *myself*."

She takes a step closer. "And you know what? If I can't have him, *no one will*." She takes a knife out from inside her jacket and plunges it into my chest.

My lungs seize. I try to gasp for air, but nothing works. I choke. The taste of blood fills my mouth before I fall. Black is creeping into my vision. I watch Crystal head through my front door before I—

## THANK YOU FOR READING!

*Enjoyed Our Little Secret? Please consider leaving a review.*

Reviews help authors more than you might think. Even just a few words make a difference and are greatly appreciated. The best place to review is whichever retailer you purchased from, but you can also consider Goodreads or BookBub.

# ACKNOWLEDGMENTS

First, I'd like to thank my husband and son for being my biggest supporters. Thank you for always believing in me and cheering me on, for holding me up on my worst days, and standing by my side on my best. I'm so blessed to have both of you. I love you to infinity and beyond.

Thank you to my editor and proofreader at My Brother's Editor for being amazing at what you do and so wonderful to work with.

And to my readers, from the bottom of my heart, thank you for your continued support and encouragement. You are the lifeblood that runs through an author's veins. You are the reason we do what we do and the reason I'm where I'm at today. I couldn't have done it without you.

Thank you for taking a chance on this book. Whether you are new to my work or are coming back for more, I truly hope you enjoyed the read.

# ABOUT THE AUTHOR

K. Lucas is a bestselling author who lives for the unexpected twist. Originally from California, she now lives in the Pacific Northwest with her husband, son, dogs, cat, and chickens. After earning a bachelor's degree in information technology, she became a homeschool mom and then a full-time author. She loves all things thrilling & chilling, and her favorite pastimes include reading, watching scary movies, and exploring nature.

**www.klucasauthor.com**

# CONNECT WITH THE AUTHOR

See K. Lucas's website for more info, signed copies, and to sign up for newsletter updates!

Website:
www.klucasauthor.com

Newsletter:
www.klucasauthor.com/newslettersignup

amazon.com/author/klucas

goodreads.com/klucas

instagram.com/author_klucas

facebook.com/author.klucas

tiktok.com/@klucasauthor

pinterest.com/klucasauthor

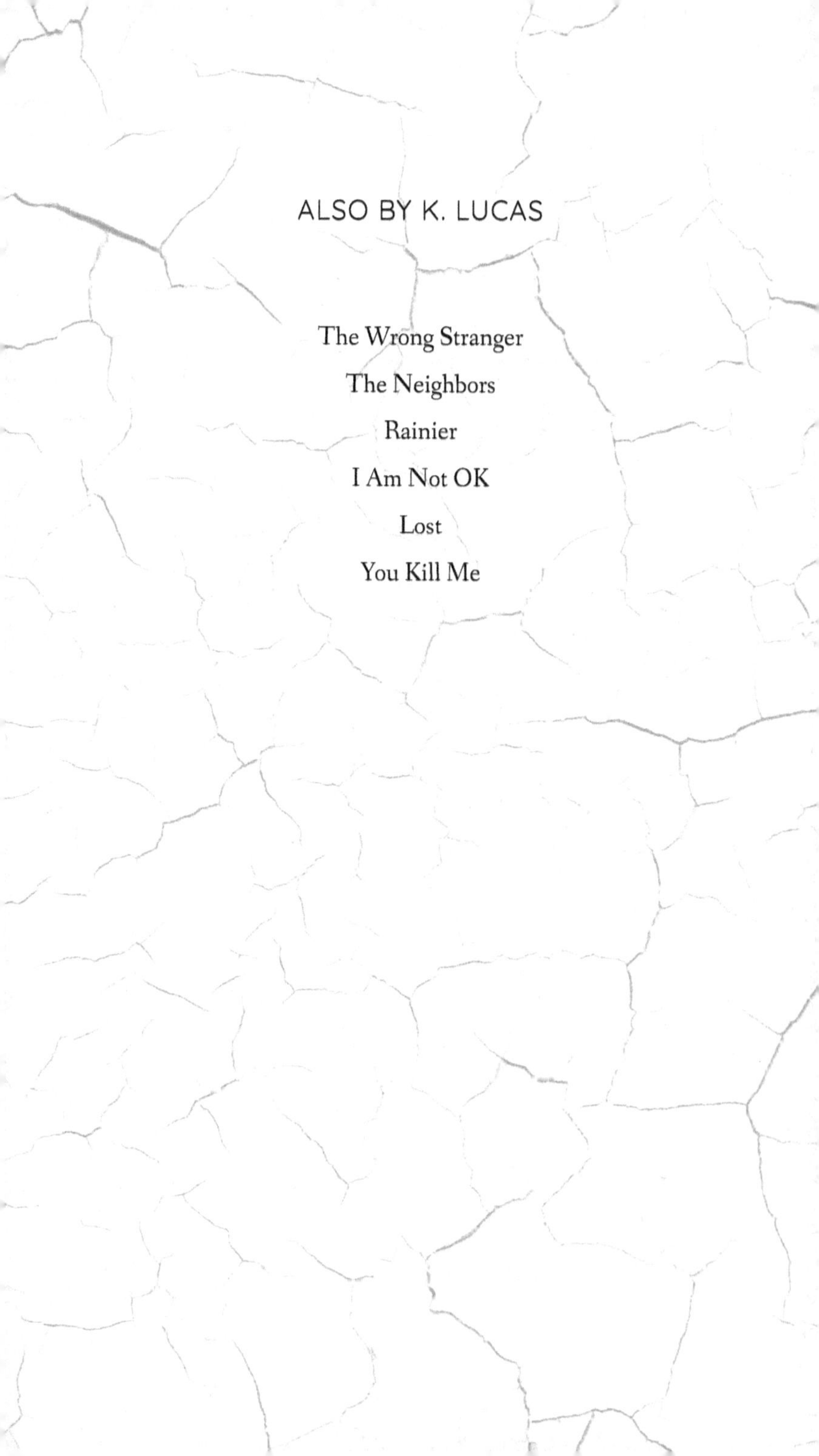



The Wrong Stranger

The Neighbors

Rainier

I Am Not OK

Lost

You Kill Me